HAREM OF FANGS

Harem of Fangs

EMMA DAWN

The characters and events portrayed in this book are fictitious. Any similarity to real persons, living or dead, is coincidental and not intended by the author.

ISBN: 1544934890
ISBN 13: 9781544934891

Note of Thanks

I would like to thank those who are taking a chance on a new author. Your support, reviews and encouragement mean a whole lot to me, more than I can ever truly thank you for. This story and those that follow are for those who believe that love can transcend the norms, and that you never know when it might jump up and bite you in the ass. Enjoy!

Chapter One

I rubbed my hands over my face, the computer screen blurring a little, the words warping into an unreadable mess. A sigh of air slid from me. "Novel isn't going to write itself," I muttered under my breath, as I stared at the blank page with nothing but a blinking cursor to show for my efforts. I just needed a break, a vacation, anything to get a chance to find my passion again.

Luke lifted his head from his spot on the couch next to me, yawned, and curled his tail around his face once more so I only saw a glimmer of his Husky-dog baby blues before they closed tightly.

"Some help you are. You're supposed to be staying awake with me, Luke." I stretched and glanced at the clock. One a.m. Deadline for final edits was tomorrow and I still had over fifty pages to go in order to wrap it up. My publisher would not be happy if I was late with the manuscript.

But my mind wasn't on the task at hand because today was an anniversary that a year ago would have had me broken and heaving sobs on the floor. Yet, here I was working on a paranormal romance, no less, with zero tears and not a single sob.

I leaned over and touched the framed picture of my ex-fiancé. "A year since you left me. Can you believe it, Mike? A whole year, and here I am, still alive. Doing better than ever without your sorry, cheating ass."

Some people called it ridiculous that I kept a picture of him. For me, though, every time I saw it, I was reminded that if he hadn't left me high and dry, I would never have gotten out of the rut my life had become. Him leaving me for that skanky, man-stealing, older than she looked and fatter than she claimed, Wanda, had shown me I still had a lot of life to live. "Just watch me, Mike. I'm going to get this book done, and I'm going to be rolling in good reviews, and readers who love me." I flicked his face with a finger, wishing it was more like a voodoo doll that would transfer the pain.

I looked away from his face, from the smile that had at one point been my entire world. A smile I thought would become a part of our future children's facial features. I shook my head and looked back to the screen. Fifty pages, I could do this.

Hands once more on the keyboard, the words began to flow. One thousand, two thousand words...ten pages, fifteen, twenty. I checked the clock. Three a.m.

I pushed to my feet and stretched my back, pressing my knuckles into my lower spine.

If not for Mike's betrayal, thirty-eight would have been my best year yet.

"No, it *was* my best year." I nodded, pushing away the hurt that still lingered, here and there. While it was an effort to build my confidence back, I'd done it with the help of my close circle of friends that consisted of my bestie, Cassie, and my little sister, Dominique.

My books had taken off under my pen name, and I'd paid off all the debt Mike and I had accrued over the years. I'd lost that extra twenty pounds I'd carried since forever, and I'd made myself try something new every other month. Skydiving, pottery, archery, karate, salsa dancing, and the list went on. I'd even ridden a donkey to the bottom of the Grand Canyon with Cassie the month before. She cursed me for it, and both of us were sore for days, but to me, it had been totally worth it.

Still, there was an emptiness that had blossomed in my chest since Mike left, and it hovered at the edges of everything I did. The belief that maybe he was right to leave me, that I wasn't worth any man's time, was still there despite the work I'd put into myself.

My cell phone buzzed with an incoming text. The phone rattled so hard, it jumped to the edge of the table, and I caught it just before it dropped to the hardwood floor.

The name at the top of the text did not surprise me, but it did make me sad. Cassie was forever drinking and texting me in the middle of the night. I wasn't the only one trying to find my way after a shitty relationship.

A frown dipped between my brows as I read the text.

At Tink's bar. Please come get me.

Like me, Cassie was no longer attached to a man. Unlike me, it had been her choice, and a smart one at that. Peter had been messing around on her for a year.

Unfortunately, the breakup had left Cassie vulnerable and a bit on the dangerous side when it came to men. Worse, she'd taken a job that, while high-paying and keeping her in top shape, was almost as dangerous as her choice in men.

She was a skydiver during the day and a karate instructor at night. Hence my lessons in both.

"Cassie, what are you doing now?" I asked as I typed a quick reply that I was on my way.

Sighing, I tucked the phone into my back pocket and headed for the stairs that led into the basement, and my little sister's suite. After Mike left, she moved in because she wanted to take care of me. At least, that was what she said.

I did my best not to point out that she was homeless at the time, and jobless, and pretty much a slug when it came to making any sort of an effort to change either of those things. All she did was sleep, which made me wonder if she was struggling with depression. Not the first time to consider that path, I found myself making a note to get her to the doctor. Even if I had to drag her.

I knocked on her door, then let myself in. "Dominique, I'm going out to get Cassie from the bar. I shouldn't be long."

"Ally?" She waved a hand at me and barely lifted her head. Her features were so close to mine, we could have been twins in our coloring. Blond hair and blue-green eyes that were sometimes labeled as turquoise. I smiled at her, the tousled look, and for a moment I could see her as a kid again. Only a few years younger than me, she was anything but a kid. But I would always be older and she would always be my responsibility.

"Yeah, that's my name," I said. "I'll be back soon, okay?"

She yawned, closed her eyes and snuggled back into the couch cushions. I rolled my eyes at her ability to just drop off like that. A talent I wished I had. I tossed a blanket over her prone form, flicked off the light beside the couch, and headed out to my car.

The drive to Tink's took a little under half an hour, and the light rain on the roads kept me doing the speed limit like a good girl. New England in the winter was dodgy at best, especially here, this close to the mountains. It wouldn't be long before we'd be knee-deep in snow, if the dropping temperatures were any indication.

Pulling up to the bar, I peered through the rain that was no longer light, but coming down in buckets that splatted my windshield. "Awesome, just flipping awesome, Cassie. Why couldn't you have done this on a summer's night?"

I foolishly had not brought a coat, thinking I had one in the front seat. That's what I got for having a garage attached to the house. I'd climbed into the car wearing nothing more than a T-shirt and loose pajama bottoms. In part, because silly me had thought Cassie would be smart enough to be waiting outside.

I was never going to learn when it came to my friend.

With a huff, I slid out of the car, threw one arm over my head and rushed toward the building. I stepped in no less than two puddles, and I cursed them both as they soaked my pant legs almost to my knees.

I hit the bar door at full speed, and flung it open wide. The heavy wooden door banged against the wall with a thunderous boom that echoed in the empty space.

Empty space? I took a step and then another, as I wiped the rain from my face. While it was late, the bar should have still had a few patrons left, a few hangers-on. Tink's never really shut down. Where was Bobby-Jo the bouncer, and Earl, the old guy who all but lived here? I didn't think either of them actually had a home, but lived in the bar itself.

Yet, they weren't here, and the place was empty. As empty as a tomb holding the secrets of the dead...I shivered and wrapped my arms around my middle.

Stupid writer brain just had to go there, didn't you? I thought.

I cleared my throat, and squared my shoulders. "Cassie, where are you?"

There was silence for a heartbeat, and then a voice that was most certainly not Cassie's answered me.

"Ahhh, so you *are* the friend she called on. Lovely; we were thinking you might not come."

The voice was velvety soft, distinctly masculine, and maybe another time, I would have thought it sexy as all get-out. But I was thirty-eight and tired of men and their stupid games, and their desire to prove how big and strong they were. I did not need this shit.

I fought not to roll my eyes. Ah, forget it, let them roll.

"Where is my friend?" I did a complete spin as I worked my way deeper into the club. The funny thing about losing Mike was that instead of feeling afraid of life as I had before, instead of turning from anything that even remotely scared me, I tended now to run toward it. Which might have explained the fancy new muscle car I was driving and the intense love of skydiving.

A part of my brain tried to tell me I was being dangerously stupid by staying in the bar, that I needed to stop moving deeper into the place. That I needed to just...stop, to turn around and run.

I couldn't seem to make my body obey my brain. Besides, Cassie was here, and she was my friend. I wasn't leaving her behind, not because my overactive imagination was placing all sorts of unhelpful images in the front of my brain.

Dead bodies.

Ghosts.

Ax murderers.

Twisted mutants come down from the hills.

Nope, I wasn't falling for my own imagination this time. My feet kept on going until I was in the middle of the dance floor. I put my hands on my hips and called out.

"Cassie, you get your ass end out here, right now, or I'm leaving without you. I mean it!"

No one answered. I mean, no one said anything. There wasn't even a response from that velvety voice from before. Instead, my answer came slowly in a physical form.

A group of men circled me from the shadows, step after step. Each was cloaked in darkness, their faces hidden by hoods or by the shadows from the few lights left on in the club.

Fear should have been racing down my spine. I should have been running for the doors, and for sure, a year past I would have been. That was the old me, though, and I was done with fear.

I arched an eyebrow and shifted my stance so I was better balanced—thank you to my whopping four karate lessons. I faced the man closest to me. "Really? This is how you want tonight to go? Because I'm telling you right now, I do not have the patience for this shit. Not tonight. Not ever. I will kick your ass and hand it to one of your friends in pieces."

The figure closest stepped forward. The velvety voice was the one from when I'd first stepped into the bar.

"Most assuredly, woman, you will fall at my feet and beg me for my manhood to pierce you."

I burst out laughing, unable to contain my mirth at what had to be the most ridiculous line of shit I'd ever heard.

"Dude, is that the best you've got, because I've heard, and read, better. And I've read a lot of super cheesy romance books. Research, you know." I took a big breath, held up a hand and pointed a single finger at him. "I do not know *what* you are on, but there will be no begging out of this pretty little mouth." I then pointed at my lips for good measure. "No more games. Where is my friend?" I did a half-turn away from him, and the other men who circled me grumbled and more than one gasped.

"Did she just deny Malcom?"

"That's not possible."

"But there it is."

A few more mutterings along those lines. I rolled my eyes and started toward the guy they named Malcom. "Listen, get out of my way, Malcom. If you aren't going to tell me where she is, I'll find her myself."

I put my hand on his chest as I got close and gave him a light shove. At least, that was the plan. He was built like a damn brick shithouse, solid and unmovable like his feet were cemented into the floor. More than that, though, was the pure shot of electricity between us that made us both suck in a sharp breath. Pretty, yes, he was very pretty with his light blond hair cut close to his head, and the blue eyes that reminded me of cornflowers. But pretty did not equate nice in my books. Nor did electrical impulses that I damn well knew were a bad idea.

"Come on, now, don't be difficult. It's late and I want to get some sleep tonight at some point." I tried to shove him again, doing my best to ignore a second flash of skin-tingling heat.

Nothing. He didn't move, not even a single inch.

I frowned. "Seriously, get the hell out of my way, man."

"Suck my balls." He whispered the words as if they would somehow seduce me on the spot, low and breathy as he leaned toward me. I will admit, my mouth dropped open a little, probably giving him the wrong idea of just what the words had done to me.

"What did you say?" I spluttered.

"I said suck my—"

I rammed my knee up and gave his balls something to think about. "Worst pickup line, ever." I threw the words at him as I shoved him—easily now—aside.

He went to the floor with a groan and the other men in the room laughed, a ripple of sound that rose and fell as it moved through them, tickling along the edge of my spine in a not-unpleasant way. I almost turned back to them.

Almost, but I contained the urge.

With a shiver, I hurried to the back where the washroom was located, assuming Cassie would be there. If not there, maybe the manager's office. The lights in the hallway that led to the washrooms were dim, and I slipped twice on spilled beer. I wrinkled my nose. Thank God, I was no longer that young and stupid to not only drink until I was completely soused, but also to think men like that douche Malcom could talk to me as if anything he said would be acceptable. What? Because he was a man? Because he had a dick and a tiny pair of marbles? *Please.*

What a complete and total shithead.

I put my hand to the washroom door and shoved it open. I saw her feet and her five-inch heels before I saw anything else. Slouched in a corner, Cassie was slumped over her cell phone. Her chest rose and fell in an even beat. I shook my head as I hurried to her side, and crouched next to her.

"Cassie, come on, hon. I'll take you home. You can stay at my place tonight, okay?" I put a hand to her face, and tipped her chin up.

Blood coated her neck. I gasped. "What happened to you?"

"Bit me. Felt so fucking good. So. Good." She whispered the words, her dark brown eyes staring at me under a haze of alcohol. "Wanted you to feel the same. You deserve to feel good, Ally. You deserve it."

My gorge rose at the sight of the blood. I pushed to my now-wobbling feet and hurried to the sink. I grabbed paper towels, went back to Cassie and pressed the wad of paper to her neck.

"We've got to get you out of here," I whispered, for the first time truly realizing the danger we could be in. A group of five men, and the two of us, one of whom was pretty much useless if it came to a fight. Not that I would be much better. Losing weight with Zumba and salsa dancing did not make one a fighter. Fit, yes. Fighting skills? Not so much.

The creak of a floorboard outside the bathroom door had me on feet in a flash. I leapt to the door and threw the deadbolt lock on it. Maybe it wouldn't be much, but it could buy us the time we needed to call the police. I dropped back to Cassie's side and took her phone, dialing 9-1-1.

The operator picked up right away. "9-1-1, what is your emergency?"

"I'm at Tink's bar with my friend. She's been cut badly on the neck..." I didn't for one minute think she'd been bitten. She'd had an unhealthy obsession with vampires for years, "and had lost a lot of blood. The men who did it are in the club still and we are locked in the bathroom."

I spoke quickly, my words as clear and concise as I could make them, and yet...

"Could you repeat that?"

"Tink's bar. Injured woman. Roving maniacs outside bathroom door." The words were about as hard as I could make them and still whisper.

The door of the bathroom suddenly shuddered as if a body had been thrown into it. I couldn't help the squeak that slipped from my lips. "Hurry. Please!"

"What bar?"

"Oh, for God's sake! Tink's bar on Henrietta Ave!"

The operator did the most unprofessional thing I could have possibly imagined in that moment, and if she'd worked for me I would have fired her on the spot.

The bitch hung up on me.

Chapter Two

The door to the bathroom shuddered twice more while I desperately tried to dial 9-1-1 again, praying I would get a different operator. Someone who would take me seriously. Someone who wouldn't just hang up on me. What a twat! Who did that? What operator hung up on someone when they were calling for help?

It was not to be, though, there was no chance to get the phone dialed again. While I fumbled with the stupid little phone, my knees in her blood on the floor, and Cassie grabbing at me with her flailing hands in a vain attempt to help, I think, the bathroom door crashed open and that shit-faced (okay, I'll admit now in the light, he was pretty flipping handsome) Malcom stood over me, still clutching his balls with one hand. "Did you truly walk away from me, woman? You dared to bust my balls and walk away?"

I glared up at him, fear and anger making me waspish and far bolder than even on a good day. "Did you seriously tell me to suck your manhood when you don't even know my name? What is wrong with you? That is not how you talk to a lady. Do you kiss your mother with that filthy, dirty, dirty mouth?" Sure. I might have been staring at said mouth a little too much, a little too long.

So, sue me, I could look. I just wouldn't touch. I wasn't that desperate.

His eyes widened with each word. "Obey me!" He spoke with such force I wondered if he was constipated. I debated offering to get him a laxative.

"Go away!" was what I settled for yelling at him. "Unless you're a doctor, in which case you can stay and help me because she's bleeding badly." I waved a hand at Cassie who mumbled in her semi-conscious state. With her unhealthy obsession with the idea that vampires could be real, I was not surprised she believed she had been bitten.

My choice of storytelling had been right up her alley, and she'd gobbled the fantasy book after book. Vampires and werewolves and witches, oh my! But I knew the difference between reality and fantasy.

Cassie did not, as evidenced by her reaction to the cut on her neck, calling it a bite. She'd been chasing a sexual high that didn't exist for years. My worst fear for her was facing me—that she'd found someone to play into her fantasy who would hurt her and leave her to die somewhere.

"You better hope to God you didn't do this to her." I glanced at Malcom while I kept pressure on the wound. "I mean it, HOPE TO GOD."

"I did not bite her. But what exactly do you think you could do to me, if I had been the one?" Malcom asked softly, his blue eyes turning dangerously dark.

I stood and jammed a single finger into the tip of his nose. "I'll cut your damn balls off myself and turn them into hacky sacks," I snapped. "Now, help me get her to my car since the damn 9-1-1 operator won't answer me."

Malcom reached past me with a speed so fast, his hand blurred. He snatched the phone and crushed it in his palm as if it were nothing more than a child's toy.

"What are you doing, you idiot!" I screamed at him, but I knew what he was doing. I knew exactly what he was doing and it freaked me out.

He was cutting us off from getting help, from getting out of here alive. I dropped back to my knees and put pressure on Cassie's neck once more, feeling her heartbeat throb under my hand. She was alive, but I had no idea for how long, or how bad the wound was. What if one of these maniacs—the other six men now peering in through the doorway—had actually bitten her? The wound would be ragged from their blunt teeth, and for sure, her neck would need stitches and care from a proper hospital and doctor. Maybe even a rabies shot, by the looks of a few of the men.

Malcom smiled at me. "Feisty, and somewhat impervious to my voice. That is interesting. The queen will want to meet you. Perhaps, you are the last."

One of the other men grunted and shook his head. "You think she's going to be bonded to one of the five?"

Malcom nodded. "Yeah, it's about the only thing that would make sense. No other reason for her to be able to ignore my call." He rubbed at his balls and squinted his eyes. "And that knee to my balls was no human blow."

I stood again and snapped the fingers of my free hand back and forth in front of his face to get his attention. "Hey. My friend needs help, not some mumbo jumbo about being bonded. If you still want a blow job, you can have one from my pencil sharpener."

Not to mention the queen comment. What queen? We lived in New England in the good old U.S. of A. No queens here. Other than those who dressed in drag on the weekends.

I blinked in mid-thought, and the world moved at a rather sudden and rapid pace that I couldn't follow. Between one moment and the next I went from standing on the floor, to being in the air, and then hung over Malcom's shoulder. I hadn't seen him move, or even take a breath. Just one minute on the dirty bathroom floor in my pj's and the next on his shoulder. Was that even possible?

I took a breath, kicked and screamed as I slammed my fists into his back, my elbow in the back of his head, bruising my funny bone and barely making him move. We walked through the club in this fashion as though it were completely normal. Then again, he wasn't exactly immune to my attempts. I angled my elbow to drive into the side of his head, snapping his head from side to side.

"If you were anyone else, I'd drain you here and be glad to watch you die." He all but hissed the words. Harder than it sounded when there was only one *s* in the sentence.

I paused in my ministrations on the back of his head and looked around for my friend. One of the other men had Cassie in his arms. She was still passed out.

"Don't you dare hurt her!" I screamed at him, shaking a fist as though I were some curmudgeonly old man on the edge of his porch, screaming at the neighborhood kids to get the hell off his lawn and stop toilet-papering his house.

"Then be still," Malcom said as he tightened his hold on my legs. "She is our security for your good behavior."

I clenched my hands into fists as I fought not to fight. I didn't want to give in, but I didn't want Cassie to be hurt either.

"What are you going to do with us?" I cringed as the words slipped from me. Like a damsel in distress, waiting for her white knight to rescue her. Bah.

"To the queen," was all he said. We stepped—okay, he stepped; I was still slung over his shoulder—out of the bar and into the now-snowing night.

"Wonderful," I muttered.

"Get rid of her car." Malcom made a motion toward *my car.*

"No! Don't you touch my car!"

One of the other men who had stringy long black hair grinned at me and jingled my keys before he slid into the driver's side. My most favorite car with the all-leather interior and the beautiful purple paint job with thick black racing stripes.

Not my car, don't let them hurt my car, I thought.

I let out low snarl. "I hate you."

"Fine by me," Malcom grumbled. "I hope I'm wrong about you, and the queen drains you."

His words made me blink. "Drains me. What is that? Some kind of euphemism?"

He snorted. "No, it's not. *Drains* means exactly what your brain thinks it means. Drains you of all your blood and bathes in it. I hope she does that exactly, and that she allows me to watch."

Now, to be fair, I was slung over his shoulder, and there had never been a time in my life that I had been prone to passing out.

Seeing as I'd just been essentially kidnapped, my favorite car stolen and likely driven into a ditch somewhere, then threatened to have all my blood drained from me, now was the time to have my moment.

My eyes rolled and I slumped, the world spinning as I fought to claw my way back to a more conscious state. Yet, it was not to be, not even after I was shoved into the dark space of a vehicle I didn't know, or when Cassie was shoved against me. If anything, the pressure to let the blank space of unconsciousness increased until I succumbed, and slumped into the far-too-cushiony seats.

My last thought was simple.

If I am going to die, I hope I can at least get in one more kick to that dipshit's balls.

Chapter Three

I came out of the cold fog of unconsciousness with a bolt, flinging my fists outward as if I would slay the dragon...Where was I? Still at the bar with Cassie? No, that wasn't right. There had been a total dick named Malcom who'd tried to command me to suck his balls.

That had to have been a dream. No man was that stupid or that arrogant.

Running water trickled at the edge of my senses, helping me ground myself, and though it did that, it also gave me the intense urge to pee.

I shuddered and a raspy breath rattled through me. I blinked and tried to see through the tangle of my dark blond hair. Carefully, I pressed my hands to the stone beneath me and pushed until I was standing on slightly wobbly legs.

That cold stone continued up the walls and to the ceiling of what could only be called a castle. A castle? In New England? I knew there were a few mansions that dated back to a bygone era, maybe that was where we were. But I didn't think so.

I rubbed a hand over my eyes and did a slow turn toward the one sound in the room. In front of me was a waterfall cascading down behind a throne that looked to be made of solid gold. Seated on the throne was a woman far younger than me, by what had to be at least twenty years. Her face was unlined, that soft skin untouched by the woes of the world, the pain of the heart, or the hurt caused by those meant to love you. Dressed in a shimmering gown of gold, the material clung to her curves. Where the throne left off and the gown began was hard to tell. Jet-black hair hung to her waist in perfect, artistic waves, and eyes the green of an emerald stared down at me.

She was stunningly beautiful.

I hated her a little bit just based on that.

She helped cement that hatred with the first words out of her mouth. Her plump lips turned downward as she stared at me.

"Why would you bring us an old hag, Malcom? She has to be almost forty. What use has she left?"

I glared up at her, my mouth filter not catching up with my brain. "Who would put a child on a golden throne and think her capable of anything other than saying stupid shit?"

Gasps rippled around the room from people I hadn't seen before. They did that creepy, ghosting in closer thing that Malcom had pulled on me at the bar. I went from being alone, standing in front of that snot-nosed, beautiful brat, to being surrounded by men, yet again.

Run away.

The thought was so strong inside my mind, I wasn't entirely sure it was mine.

I frowned harder. Mind reading was not real. Vampires were not real. This was not real. I was in some sort of dream—

"It is not a dream, Allianna."

I gasped and spun toward the man who'd spoken. "How the hell do you know my name?" Because Allianna was a name I'd legally given up years ago. Too long, too hard to spell, it didn't fit well on book covers. Allianna was just too much for me. I was little old plain Ally Swift and happy to be so.

The man in question took another step. Unlike Malcom, he made no effort to hide his face from me, and I will admit that I struggled to breathe as I took him in. Eyes of the darkest blue, and hair the color of mahogany, lips that looked as though he'd just finished laughing but with a hint of sadness on the edge of them. His face was narrow, coming to a squared-off chin covered in a slight stubble that was shades lighter than the hair on his head. He wore a black button-down shirt open at the throat and black slacks that clung to his very, very, very nice lower half.

With effort, I drew my eyes back up to his face and managed to croak out a few words. "Who are you?"

"I am known as Preacher." He tipped his head ever so slightly. "And I am your first."

"First what?" My brain didn't like this game. Going from fear, to confusion, on to a burning lust so hot, I was pretty sure I was no longer wearing any panties because one look at him had melted them off, and then back to confusion made my head hurt.

Preacher smiled, showing off perfectly white teeth and...a pair of fangs. Fangs. Real fangs. No, fake fangs.

21

"They are not fake, Allianna, they are real, as this is real." He took a step toward me, then another and another, and the tension between us ratcheted up at a speed I could not understand. My heart was pounding and my skin prickled with a need I hadn't felt since Mike had left me and broken my heart.

Preacher lifted a long-fingered hand and ran the tips of his fingers down the side of my face with the most careful of touches, as if I were something precious. "Come with me, I will explain everything."

I let him take my hand, let him begin to lead me away until that twat on the throne snorted. "She will never take my place. Not if you worked with her a thousand years, Preacher, would she be what you want her to be. Like the others, she will die."

From his hand, I felt the slightest of tremors, which meant the shot she threw at me was meant for him too. I found myself squeezing his hand in a small attempt at solidarity. I half-turned, but spoke to Preacher.

"Funny, did you hear something? For a just a split second there, it sounded like a baby crying." I smiled as I spoke. Maybe I'd lost my mind, because I'd just been threatened with my life and it had done no more than amuse me.

Preacher tightened his hold on my hand and then we were moving so fast my feet skimmed the floor, like I was flying as he drew me away from what could only be called a throne room.

"You should not push her like that. She could kill you if she was so inclined." He glanced at me, his eyes softening, and the color seemed to soften with the emotion on his face.

"Here, come and I will explain why you are here, and what...I am to you, being your first."

We stood in front of a large door strapped with metal bindings, as though being held together more by metal than the wood. He touched the door and it swung inward. The room in front of me was warm, and for the first time, I realized how cold I was. A shiver ran down my body and I rubbed my arms.

"Ah, perhaps we should get you some dry clothes and increase your temperature." Preacher didn't let go of me, but drew me deeper into the room by my hand. The door closed on its own behind us with a soft click. The room seemed a cocoon of safety and warmth, every breath of air against my skin felt like Preacher was touching me. Which was stupid and silly because I'd met the man with the fake fangs only moments before. I refused to think of him as a vampire. I was not Cassie.

Thoughts of my friend sent a shot of shame through me. "Wait. What happened to my friend? Where is she?"

Preacher smiled and I thought for a moment the breath in my body might flee and I'd die right there on the spot, his mouth and face were so dang delectable. Cover models be damned, this dude was the real deal.

"She is in the hospital wing being taken care of by the very best doctors. Do not be afraid for her. She will go home and remember none of this."

A breath of relief slid through me.

He tipped his head to the side. "You trust my words?"

I shrugged and a small laugh escaped me. "Crazy, I know, but I feel like we've met before. Or that I've known you before. I think I can trust you."

He closed the distance between us, and cupped my face with his hands, splaying his fingers over my cheeks.

"I did not want to feel this. I did not think it possible, though I have been warned for years." He dipped his head so our foreheads touched. He drew in a shuddering breath. My hands were on his forearms, clinging to him, holding him to me. I swallowed with some difficulty.

"What happens now?"

"I need to get you warm, and then I will explain everything." His words were a whisper that floated out and landed on my lips, slid down my neck and curled over my skin, tightening my body with a luscious need. I dared to look into his eyes, to see what was there, if it was just me slowly being consumed with want.

His dark blue eyes were nearly black with desire. "I need to get you warm."

"You already said that," I pointed out, unable to stop the stupid smile that slid over my lips. "Is there a shower or a tub?"

A part of my brain yelped at me that this was beyond foolish, stupid, dangerous. It was downright ridiculous. I was basically inviting a man I'd met only moments before, a man who believed he was a vampire no less, to have a shower with me.

Ah, what the hell, you only live once, and he was the finest piece of ass I'd ever seen in my entire life. Besides, I wasn't entirely sure this wasn't a dream, and if it was a dream, I could do anything I wanted and it would be safe. I would wake up, and have an amazing memory to look back on.

I arched an eyebrow and stepped back, letting my hands slide down his arms to his fingers. I couldn't help but notice the size of his hands, wondering what magic they could send sizzling over my skin. I pursed my lips. "You game, or am I showering by myself?"

His eyebrows shot up and a smile tickled at the edges of his mouth. "Game, very, very game, Allianna."

He slipped toward me, catching me up in his arms, one hand going to my ass, the other holding me tightly around the waist. The hand on my ass dug in with a delicious strength, massaging at the flesh while pressing me against him as he walked through the main room.

Distantly I took note of the bed, the silk sheets, the two chests on either side of the bed, the open closet full of clothing. I think perhaps I was making a weak attempt to keep my wits about me. It wasn't working all that well as my eyes kept sliding back to Preacher's face.

My interest in the room faded as we reached the bathroom, though bathroom wasn't quite the right word. Perhaps spa would be a better, more accurate descriptor. The intricately tiled room was done in black and gold, from the floor up to the walls and across the ceiling. The designs in gold, swirls and the like, shimmered in the candles lit throughout. The room was as big as any master bedroom, and in fact, there was a lounge on one side I could easily sprawl on and have a nap. Though sleeping was most certainly not on my mind at that particular moment.

Dreaming, this was all a dream, therefore I could do whatever I wanted.

"Not a dream, Allianna," Preacher said. "I promise you this is as real as anything you've ever experienced."

I slowly turned in his arms as he lowered my feet to the floor. "You keep saying that, but there is nothing to make me believe this is real. Like *really* real. Even this room." I swept my hand outward. "It's ridiculous. There isn't even an attempt to make it look like a normal bathroom."

The tub had to be big enough for six people, easily, with room to spare. More like a hot tub, only I could see it wasn't. The tub looked fantastic, but I'll admit, it was the shower that had my attention.

It was easily ten foot by ten foot with multiple shower heads, a wide bench along the back, and better yet, handles and foot holds all over the wall. My breath tightened in my chest and my nipples hardened with the mere thought of how many positions I could hold while Preacher slipped into me, while he touched me and put his hands all over my body, in my body—

"Yes," he growled. "Yes, to all of it."

I whimpered softly, anticipation shooting through me like a bolt of pure orgasmic pleasure that made my knees tremble. Preacher hadn't even truly touched me yet. We hadn't kissed, hadn't taken off a shred of clothing, and I was on the cusp of coming for him *right there.*

His mouth was at my ear. "Yes. To all of it, yes, a thousand times, Allianna. I will make you sob for mercy before this night is over."

"You don't want my confession, Preacher?" I couldn't help myself.

He chuckled and nipped the edge of my ear. "Only if you are on your knees."

"Oh fuck." I whispered and locked my knees to keep standing.

A laugh rolled through him. "That *is* the plan, my lady."

He turned me slowly, his hands never leaving my body as he spun me to face him.

Chapter Four

Preacher and I stood, staring at each other, and for a moment, I just marveled at how damn beautiful he was, that he was there with me and wanted me. Whatever fears I'd had about where I was, or why I was there, dissolved under the growing need to be with the man in front of me. To feel him inside me and complete that piece of my life I suddenly knew only he could fill.

A dream, and I would live it to the fullest before I woke. Mike...thank God Mike had left me so I could live this moment.

"He was a fool to walk away from you." Preacher drew a slow breath and let it out as his hands went to my shoulders, then slid down to my hands. I held perfectly still as he grasped the bottom edge of my shirt and pulled it upward, inch by delicious inch. I lifted my arms, let him take the thin, still-damp shirt from me. My first thought was that at least I'd put on a bra not falling apart at the seams. My second thought was that I wished I had some sexy lingerie.

"You don't need it." He leaned in and placed his mouth against the edge of my jawline. "You don't need a single thing to make you more beautiful than you already are, Allianna."

His lips and stubble grazed the curves and lines of my face as his hands slid around my back, slipping under the edges of my bra. A tremble started under my skin, a shiver of heat and lightning that made my breath catch and my thoughts melt away into nothing. Or almost nothing.

"It does up in front," I whispered.

"I don't plan to unclasp it," he whispered back. He wrapped his fingers around either side of the bra strap at the back, and with a sharp yank, snapped it in half. "You won't be needing it tonight."

"Right," I said. A gasp escaped me as the bra fell to the floor and the cool air drifted around my nipples. They perked right up, begging to be touched.

Preacher's nostrils flared, his jaw worked and I saw him swallow hard. I dared to lift my fingers, and run one over his bottom lip. "Please, tell me you aren't nervous."

His lips twitched. "Perhaps, a little."

"Maybe I can help you with that." I reached up and slid my hands around the back of his head, and pulled him to me. I planted my lips on his with a hard, bruising kiss. I slid my tongue into his mouth, darting, touching, teasing him. Daring him to keep up with me. My body was singing with desire, with a need so strong I wanted to both wrap my legs around him, and hold him tight to me so I could feel every inch of him.

I was no teenager on her first go-around of the carousel. I knew what I liked, and I knew what I wanted, and right now nothing filled my mind like the thought of being skin on skin with Preacher. To feel every part of him on me, in me, with me.

If he could really read my mind, as seemed to be the case, this was about to get interesting in the most delightful of fashions.

I couldn't resist flicking my tongue up and touching the tip of it to one of his fangs. A groan slid from him and he clutched at me. "Don't. I won't last a minute if you play with them."

I blinked up at him, breathing hard, my mind a bit of a mess with haze of desire clouding it. "What?"

"They are...sensitive. Touching them is incredibly erotic, and will bring me far too fast." He struggled to get the words out.

He didn't give me much time to consider what would happen next. He pulled me tightly to him, grinding his hips against mine so his rock-hard cock pressed against my panties, straining the thin material.

I couldn't help but arch my back, lifting my upper body as an offering to his mouth and hands, while thrusting my own hips harder against his length. I rubbed my body against his, feeling the slow burn of need rolling through me from every contact point.

God, I wanted this man, wanted every bit of him.

He took the offer. His mouth descended on the top of my breast, and he ran his tongue across the skin in a hot, wet lick that traveled around the edge of my breast and over the nipple, drawing a long low groan from my mouth. He blew out a breath of hot air, tracing the wet path of his tongue, sending a trickle of icy-hot shivers to my already aching, wet pussy.

I clung to him, unable to do anything but let him have his way with me. Let him touch me and tease me into a state of desire so strong my body thrummed with it.

He moved to the other breast, licking his way across, sucking at the skin, the stubble of his chin brushing against the sensitive flesh, sending shots of pleasure through me with each movement.

Painfully slow, he made his way back to a nipple, and sucked it into his mouth. With a flick of his tongue, he rolled the nipple around, and around, tugging and suckling over and over, bringing my body to a quivering mess of need and want.

My breath came in soft sighs and gasps of pleasure as he moved back to the first nipple, and took as much of my breast into his mouth as he could.

Under my hands his skin was hot, and his muscles tense with holding himself back. I wanted more of him, all of him.

The tips of his fangs coursed along the edge of my tit as he drew back, and once more flicked and tugged on the nipple. His free hands swept downward to the edge of my pajama bottoms. I thought he'd take the soft cotton fabric pants off with the same vigor as he'd removed my bra.

No, this was far more delicate. He slid his hand into my pants, to the edge of my panties, one finger tucking under the lacy seams at the top, tickling and teasing his way down between my legs, a preview of what, I hoped, was to come. His teeth and lips didn't slow their tugging and tasting of my breasts, moving from one nipple to the other, taking the pressure up a notch each time until the cusp of pleasure and pain hovered at the edge of my senses. A harder nip and I gasped, arching into his mouth, letting him completely take my weight on his arm holding me across my lower back.

"Please, don't stop." I groaned the words and shamelessly spread my legs for him, all but begging him to touch me. My clit ached, my panties were soaked through, and again, he'd barely started with me. I wanted to blame it on being so long since the last time I'd been good and royally taken to bed, but I couldn't. I'd never felt like this before.

I'd *written* scenes like this, absolutely. My books carried more than one tangling of limbs that left both parties breathless and in awe of each other and what they could do. But that was fantasy, and I was...I was living this.

This was sensation overload. Jet lag in the bedroom. I didn't know where I was, I didn't care, I just wanted to dive deeper into this pleasure and let it take me over, drown me, whatever it wanted as long as Preacher didn't stop.

Preacher's hands and mouth left me as suddenly as they'd started, and I slid to the floor, onto my knees, breathing hard. He turned and looked into the main room.

A voice I didn't know called out, "Did you tell her yet, Preach?"

The new voice made me squeak and I grabbed at Preacher, dousing my desire like a bucket of cold water. Who the hell was busting in on us?

Preacher flexed both hands at his sides, his head snapping around. "I'm trying, Wick. Get out of here."

"Just be sure to tell her, old chap. I'd like a chance, too."

Preacher slammed the door shut and laughter floated through it.

"Who is Wick?" I blinked up at Preacher, once more trying to bring myself back to reality.

He held out a hand to me and helped me stand. "He's my brother, of sorts. We were turned by the same old vampire. The previous queen, to be exact."

"Oh, so are you like vampire royalty then?"

He laughed and shook his head. "No. Let us talk of things of that nature later. Right now, I'd much rather taste every piece of you."

I opened my mouth and immediately closed it. I was not going to try and stop him from doing exactly what I'd wanted since he'd first touched me.

He stood in front of me and slowly unbuttoned his shirt, sliding it off his lean shoulders and letting it fall to the floor. Next came his pants, and God alive and all that was holy, he was not wearing any underwear and his cock was damn glorious.

Not a word I'd have thought for a hard-on, but there it was. Curving upward, pointing right at his belly button, smooth with a bead of moisture on the tip, just waiting for me. I moved to slide my pajama bottoms off, and he lifted a hand. "No, I'll do that."

He stepped forward and dropped to his knees in front of me. He tipped his head and looked up at me from under long dark lashes. He hooked his fingers into the top of the pants and slowly slid them down over my thighs, leaving them to puddle at my feet.

My light pink panties on the shimmering see-through side, soaked with my need for him, were all that stood between him and me.

His hands were on my hips and he leaned his face in and brushed his cheek against my panties, the stubble sticking through the material, tickling my skin. Slowly, ever so slowly, he pulled my panties down to join my pajama bottoms where they lay.

"So, beautiful, so perfect." He looked at me as he spoke, not my pussy, which was a nice change. Always good to have a man speak to you, and not to your tits and pussy.

I smiled down at him and he laughed.

"You are something else, Allianna. Even now, your laughter sparkles through your mind."

I shrugged one shoulder. "I can't help it."

"Don't try to. I love hearing your thoughts. They are a balm to my own mind."

He put his lips to the top of my bikini line and laid a gentle kiss. "Do you trust me?"

"Yes." The word slid from me before I could catch it, before I could think better of it. Mike had been a pig with me, but Preacher was all but worshipping my body, treating me like I was something precious and delicate.

He opened his mouth and pressed it against my pussy through the thin cotton, the heat and moisture of his mouth cutting through it. I grabbed a handful of his mahogany hair and held his head and mouth tightly to me, the heat of his mouth and tongue sending a flurry of shivers through me. My pussy convulsed as I flung my head back and let the sensations wash upward from my center, like a storm circling outward, touching every part of me.

He pulled the panties to one side, exposing my wet lips. "Beautiful." He groaned the word a heartbeat before he dipped his tongue between my folds, searching for my clit. I groaned, clutching him harder, urging him on.

With sure, smooth strokes, he found his way to my aching center, his tongue circling around and around, teasing it into a throbbing heartbeat all its own.

"Please—" I didn't know what I was begging for, for him to finish or to never stop. Maybe some of both. I wanted this to last forever, to die in the moment and let this be my heaven.

The slow, sure strokes of his tongue grew faster, and faster, pressing deeply between my folds the growing answer in my body demanding to be the center of his attention. My hips rocked in time with his movements. This was a storm I was riding, a storm I wanted to burst open over me, and let me scream my pleasure to the sky.

I gasped as he slid two fingers into my pussy, flicking the tips of them forward, finding my G-spot with an ease I didn't think possible. He pressed against it, stroking up and down the cushiony devil that had before always eluded me and my partners. Another groan slid from my lips as the curling pleasure tightened once more, and I struggled not to break apart into pieces. I wanted to ride this, more than anything.

Preacher's tongue and fingers moved in time with one another, stroking, demanding I give over my climax.

The building pressure in my clit and G-spot had me gasping for breath, and my hips thrusting toward him involuntarily. I literally could not control my own body any longer. Preacher was the one I wanted, the one I'd waited for.

The orgasm burst over me like a thunderclap followed by a rain shower between my legs, the scream leaping from my lips, a lightning bolt of release. Shivers ran through me as my pussy convulsed over and over, wanting more of this man, needing more of him.

Slowly, the pleasure eased and I realized I was against the cool tile wall of the shower, Preacher still on his knees in front of me. I stared down at him, my chest heaving as I worked to catch my breath.

"Wow," I whispered. He grinned up at me.

"Yes, that was rather wow. Shall I continue warming you?" He leaned over me and flicked on the shower heads. Water streamed down on all sides of us, cold and hot coming from different heads. I squealed as a cold stream hit my left side.

Preacher caught me and moved us so we were under a rain shower of barely warm water. It could have been a waterfall in the jungle if not for the black and gold tiles.

He bent his head. "Again?"

I stared up at him, my heart hammering once more. "Yes."

His lips descended on mine as he lifted me in his arms. I wrapped my arms, then legs around him, feeling the pressure of his cock pressing against my still-throbbing center. The last of the convulsions of my body from the orgasm were not even completely gone when he pressed his tip to me.

I shimmied my hips trying to get closer, trying to draw him in. Whatever world this was, dream, reality, or otherwise, I knew I didn't want to leave anytime soon.

A low rumble of pleasure rolled from him and through me. He pried one of my hands from around his back, and placed it on one of the handles on the wall. Understanding, I let go with the other hand and found another grip on the other side. Next was a foot, and I set it in a groove in the wall, leaving just one leg hooked over his hip, and easy access.

I couldn't help the laugh that slipped from me. "Who thought up this place? I'm not complaining, but seriously? This is amazing."

Preacher nodded. "It is. It was designed for pleasure."

"No shit," I said.

He pressed against me, his tip pushing past my folds, sliding over my clit to the heart of my pussy. I groaned as he dipped in an inch and then out, dipped in two inches and then out. He kept one hand splayed on the wall behind me, and the other held my leg hooked around his hip, clutching me at the base of my ass.

Deeper and deeper, he pushed, taking his time, though he had no need. "I'm not a virgin. You don't have to go slowly," I breathed, unable to make my words any louder as my body began to spasm around his length.

"I don't want to hurt you," he said. "I'm...longer than many."

"Good deal, I'll let you know if we get to a hurting point." I leaned in and bit him on the shoulder, drawing him closer yet, bringing his length deeper into me. I held him with my teeth and he groaned.

"I will not last."

I bit him harder, and he thrust deeply into me, the tip of his cock touching the edge of my womb. I could feel every inch of him and it was indeed as glorious as I'd first thought. He pulled out and slid back in, trying to slow. I could feel him trying to control the pace. I let go of him with my mouth.

"Preacher, fuck me."

The command seemed to snap through him and he blinked up at me, his eyes shocked, but also...excited. He leaned into me, his mouth on mine in a frenzy of lips and tongues as he drove himself into me, over and over.

I'd never climaxed during sex before, and I doubted it would happen now, but the aftershocks of my previous orgasm still whispered at the edges of my body, and slowly I curled toward that glittering peak. Reaching for it with my entire body.

Preacher dropped his mouth to the top of my left breast, then to the nipple as he found a steady, hard rhythm that had my back slapping against the tile with each thrust. I arched back as best I could, trying both to offer my body up and hold him close at the same time. My own climax waited for me, just at the edge of all this pleasure. Just a breath too far away.

I didn't mind really. The feeling of him inside of me, of his skin on mine and the rough stubble of his face on my breasts was certainly its own pleasure. I let the sensations wash over me, let myself feel every inch of him that touched me, let my mind revel in the feeling of his lips and tongue against my skin, of his cock deep inside of me.

All of this, all of this was what I wanted.

His speed peaked as he climbed to his own climax. His breath came in gasps as he fought to keep his mouth on my nipple. I took a chance, let go of one of the handles and brought his face to mine for a kiss. I wanted to feel connected to him everywhere, to know that we were together.

I slid my tongue over his right fang, up one side and down the other as though it were another appendage I would like to get my mouth on.

He groaned as he came, his body giving the last few bucks of pleasure as he collapsed against me, pinning me to the wall. I dropped my hands to his upper back and rested my head against his.

We were silent for almost a minute as the water pounded down around us, hot and cold splatters catching the curves of my body.

"Preacher?"

"Hmm." He slowly lifted his head, his eyes nothing short of dazed.

"You're pretty good at that."

A laugh erupted from him, full-bodied and so sudden, I had the feeling he didn't do it often. Apparently, I wasn't the only one.

The doorway opened and a head pushed in. Jet-black hair and even darker eyes panned over our entwined bodies.

"Preacher, don't tire her out." He grinned at me, eyeing me up. "I get her next."

Chapter Five

From where I was pushed against the shower wall, I stared at the—I'll admit, gorgeous, gorgeous man with his exotic looks, and long dark hair—intruder and let my gaze harden into a glare. "What the hell? I am no whore to be passed around." I was not going to be that woman. I'd been cheated on; there was no way I was doing that to anyone else. I knew the pain it caused to have someone throw you aside for another.

The intruder's eyes opened wide, and his eyebrows shot up. "Shit, he really didn't tell you yet? I thought he was just kidding—"

"I was somewhat preoccupied." Preacher started to pull away from me and I clung to him.

"Hey. You're all I've got covering me, right now."

He stepped away despite my protests, leaving me there still half-clinging to the tile wall, my body still trembling with aftershocks and a climax I'd just missed out on. With the last of my energy, I reached out and grabbed his shoulders, leaping for his back, forcing him to carry me.

He didn't stumble but he did pause and turn to look at me. "What are you doing?"

"I really don't need to be showing what God gave me to a man who just walked in on us while we were getting it on."

Preacher's eyes shuttered, hiding his emotions from me, but I caught the tail end of them. Sadness. "This is Wick. He was the one pestering us earlier."

"Earlier, Preach! It's been over an hour," Wick said as he let himself all the way into the spa bathroom. Though not as tall as Preacher, he was lean, and I could see by the way he moved, the man had some serious muscle under his clothes.

I blinked over the edge of Preacher's shoulder. "Hello, Wick. Nice to meet you. Now if you don't mind, I'd like to get some clothes on. So, whatever you were thinking about sharing me with Preacher is off the table. I'm not that kind of girl."

Besides, I really needed to check on Cassie. While I trusted Preacher, probably far more than I should have for the time I'd known him, I still wanted her to see I was okay.

Wick put both hands on his hips and pursed his lips as though deep in thought. "Preach, Preach, you are making this harder on all of us. I thought we agreed to try and do this right this time."

I frowned at him, lifting my head a little so he could get the full extent of my irritated gaze. "Making this harder on whom?"

Wick rolled his eyes, stepped back, and leaned against the wall. He stretched his legs out in front of him, so casual. I couldn't help myself from staring. There was a strange tingle down my spine that wrapped around me and pushed me in his direction. I clung harder to Preacher's back.

"See, she's drawn to me, too. She's the one," Wick said.

"I can see that," Preacher said, and I recalled very suddenly his ability to read my mind. Perhaps that wasn't the great thing I'd thought it was. I swallowed hard. "I can look. That doesn't mean I'm going to touch. I'd have to be dead not to notice him."

Again, I'd been cheated on. I wouldn't put Preacher through that for the world.

"This is not cheating, Allianna," Preacher said.

"I'm not sleeping with him," I said.

Preacher pried me off his back and handed me a thick black towel. I wrapped it around my body, tucking it under my arms. "Preacher, talk to me, please. What is wrong?"

"Nothing's wrong." He shook his head. "I only hoped to have you to myself a little longer. Selfish of me," he held up a hand to Wick, "I know, but there it is. To be just a man bedding a beautiful woman without any interruptions or ulterior motives."

"We didn't even get that," I pointed out.

Wick winked at me, and my heart rate shot up. Nothing I could do about that. I looked away, to Preacher again. If this was one of my books, what would my heroine do? If she was a tough chick, she wouldn't even have let Preacher go as far as he had. But this wasn't a scenario for a tough girl. This was my scenario, and I was the funny girl. At least, I thought I was.

"Spit it out, Preacher. I'm not getting any younger, being the hag of nearly forty that I am." I tightened my hold on the towel and lifted my chin.

Preacher grabbed a towel for himself. "I suppose the others are waiting?"

"Yup, they want to meet her." Wick grinned at me and blew me a kiss. "Come on out and meet the boys, Allianna."

Preacher followed Wick out of the bathroom, leaving me standing there like a half-frozen, totally bedraggled statue. Meet the boys. Why did I get the feeling this was not just a meet and greet for some of Preacher's friends? Wick seemed to think he was going to have some sort of shot with me.

But I...I was with Preacher. Wasn't I?

I pressed my fingers to my closed eyes and tried to think around the hormones and smell of sex that still lingered on the air. Quietly, I spoke to myself. "If this was one of your books, there would be a simple explanation. Maybe something to do with that twat who called herself a queen when you first got here. A plot to kill her maybe." I couldn't help the nervous laugh that slipped from me because I knew if this wasn't all real, I was truly slipping.

I'd gone down a rabbit hole I wasn't sure I wanted to climb back out of. Not if Preacher was here. Madness for a man like that was totally worth it.

I toweled off my hair and slid my bottoms and top on. I was not meeting with anyone in nothing but a towel. Bad enough that Wick had interrupted us.

I went to the bathroom door and peeked out. I counted four men in the room, all of them lounging as if they owned the place.

Preacher still had only the black towel that matched mine wrapped around his lean hips as he stood by the door, propped against the wall on his one arm. Pensive, he didn't look happy with whatever this situation was. I wanted to go to him and smooth away the worries in his brows.

Wick stood to the left of him, almost like they were guarding the door.

The other two men stood with their heads together in low conversation.

One was about as blond as one could be without having white hair. Tied back in a loose braid, the hair hung to his rather tight ass. I couldn't see his face, but I could guess if Wick and Preacher were any indication, he'd be as beautiful and breathtaking as any man I'd ever seen.

The last one was taller than Preacher and dressed in nothing but a pair of loose-fitting, cream-colored bottoms. His chest was bare, and so smooth, he had to have been waxed. His eyes flicked up and caught me looking. Green eyes the color of a jaguar's.

I had the urge to tuck back behind the door, but I refused to cower. I pushed the door open and stepped through.

"Preacher, are you going to tell me what's going on here?" I lifted my chin and indicated to each of the other men with the flick of a hand. "Or am I going to have to beat it out of you?"

I meant the words as a joke, but the other men reacted as if I'd uttered a serious threat. They shifted their stances and whatever kindness or interest that had been in their eyes was gone in a flash.

Preacher shook his head. "She is joking, brothers. She does not have a mean bone in her body."

"'Cept for your mean bone, eh, brother?" That was the blond. He turned and flashed brilliant baby blues the color of the summer sky at me. Wick let out a laugh, as did the blond, but it was the blond I couldn't look away from.

I swallowed hard, an image of him over me, his skin and mouth against mine so vivid that I actually stumbled back a few feet.

"Good God, what is wrong with me?" I put a hand to my head. I mean, I had a good libido, like any hotheaded almost-forty-year-old with a new lease on life. But even for me, this was ridiculous.

Preacher let out a sigh. "There is nothing wrong with you, Allianna. Please, sit. Have something to drink, and I will explain what is happening."

"Where the hell am I supposed to sit?" I threw the question at him. "The bed?"

He nodded. "If you like."

"No, that's the problem. I would like it a little too much, and I have a feeling if I did it right now, in about ten seconds I'd have four other bodies joining me. What is wrong with me?" I backed away, toward the sanctuary of the bathroom. For the first time, I was afraid. Not for my life, but because it was as though I had no control over myself. Something I was not used to in the least.

"Give me that." Wick snatched a flask from a small side table next to the door and brought it over. He handed it to me and our fingers touched. A flash of heat shot through me. I closed my eyes, swaying where I stood. Wick stepped closer, his mouth against my ear. "Drink up, love. Drink up and come for me."

I shivered, the double entendre of his words working a wicked magic over my body, the way my nipples hardened against the thin shirt as if begging for him right there. A drink sounded good right about then.

Shaking, I brought the flask to my mouth and tipped it back.

He planted a kiss on the hollow of my throat, shocking me in the loveliest of ways with the wet moisture of his lips and tongue. Shocking me more was the fact that I didn't pull away first.

He stepped back. "You were right, Preacher. She's a sweet one."

It took all I had to keep drinking. Both because of his unexpectedly gentle kiss, and the fire in the whiskey I drank down. The heat of the drink was like a literal balm to my soul, sweet and hot like a cinnamon candy.

I lowered the flask and a slight buzz rolled through my veins immediately. "That wasn't just whiskey, was it?"

Wick gave me a wicked grin. "Nah, it's an upper. It will keep you awake without any negative side effects for six days. You won't have to eat or drink either, so no worries there."

I gasped, choking on a little of the whiskey flavor still in my mouth. "Six days?"

"Yes." Preacher stepped forward. "That is the time limit."

I was shaking head to foot, unable to contain the strangeness anymore, even my rather wild and accepting writer's brain. A hand curled around me from the side and I leaned into the body. The green-eyed vampire guided me to the bed and sat me down.

"Allianna, do you need a moment?" He crouched in front of me and I had to sit on my hands to keep from reaching out to run my fingers through his hair. On the edge of auburn, it wasn't quite red, but had flickers, here and there.

"Tell me from the beginning what is going on," I said. "All of it. I'm not a child. I will not fall apart, but trust me when I tell you that if I have to guess, my brain will make this far worse than it probably is."

The other three men turned to look at Preacher. He nodded. "This underground castle is home to the queen of vampires. She is ruthless and deadly, and she is the only female amongst us. Vampires work more like a hive with workers being the men, and the queen being...serviced. She is also the only one who can create a new vampire."

I nodded for him to go on. So far so good. This was sounding like an interesting book, but I could handle it.

Preacher didn't draw closer and I wanted nothing more than for him to do exactly that. Of the four here, I knew him the best. I snorted to myself. I suppose that wasn't saying much.

Preacher gave me a soft smile, hearing my thoughts, no doubt.

"No mind reading with her. That's cheating," Wick said, giving Preacher a shove. Preacher shrugged.

"You have your gifts, I have mine." He paused, then went on. "Every one hundred years, there is an opening for a shift in power. An offering comes about, a chance, if you will, for a new queen to take over. One hundred years ago, our creator Lillianna was removed from the throne and the current queen took over."

I swallowed hard. "Okay." I could guess at where they were going with this and I didn't like it. "Tell me what that has to do with me."

"You are one of the potential queens," he said.

"Why me? Wait, there are others?"

Preacher nodded. "Five new potential queens are offered up every one hundred years. If they are not worthy, the current queen remains in state. You are the last of the five for this period." He paused. "As to *why* you, that is more complicated. Certain family bloodlines have always been drawn to the supernatural. I would guess that is also why you write what you write."

I could believe that. My stories had always been deep into the world of the fae, magic, and red-hot sex.

"And those other potential queens offered up, as it were?" I arched an eyebrow. "Should I guess what happened to them?"

"Dead," Wick said. "Killed and drained of their blood."

Preacher glared at him but I nodded. "Okay, that's what I would have guessed."

Another of the men, the green-eyed vampire to be exact, tucked an arm around my waist. "We knew you were to come to us, your name so like our creator's that it was nothing short of fate."

I glanced at him and away, careful to not be caught in his jeweled gaze. "And you are?"

"King." He bowed his head, and again I kept my hands under my butt to keep from grabbing him.

"Subtle, that," I murmured.

He chuckled. "Prince was already taken."

"Sure, I'll believe that when pigs fly." I rolled my eyes and the four men laughed with me.

I shivered. "Okay, so queen bee needs to be overthrown so I don't get killed? That's about it?"

"Not quite," Preacher said. "You must choose a first mate. The one you will twine your life with, who you will defend our hive with at your side."

I looked from Preacher, to Wick, to King, and to the blond. "I need a name," I said.

He flashed me a grin with perfect white teeth and fangs that seemed bigger than Preacher's even. "Celt, lassie. You can call me Celt."

The Irish burr in his voice literally arched my back, and I fell back to the bed as a swirling orgasm slipped up and through me. It spilled through my limbs and I let it, didn't fight it an inch as it coursed through my skin, and shot through my clit as though he had touched me and not just used his words.

King caught me as I writhed under the pleasure of his voice, as I moaned through it, my body shaking as the edges soothed away any concern I might have had, at least for a brief few seconds.

"Celt, knock it off. We need her of sound mind so she understands the gravity of the situation," Preacher growled.

The four of them argued as I lay against King's warmth, reveling in the orgasm that had literally come out of nowhere. Slowly, my breathing returned to normal and I blinked up at the ceiling. Vampires were warm, their bodies soft and hot like any human. That was a new one to me, but then this was reality, not some made-up world. Who knew how many things had been wrong in books?

Licking my lips, I sat up, my body not wanting to do anything but lie back and let one of the men—hell, at this point, I didn't even care which one—take me for a ride to ramp up that sensation curling through me. It was not to be. A hammering on the main door snapped all five of our heads to the side.

"Shit. He's here. I thought you said you stalled him!" Wick ran for the door as it was flung open, a curling of icy air whipping in ahead of the vampire in the doorway.

I rolled to my side and peered between Preacher and Celt as they stood between me and whoever had come through the door. King tugged me back against his chest, his arm over me in a decidedly protective manner.

"Who is that?" I tipped my head to him.

"That is Spartan." King let out a sigh. "Brother number five."

Chapter Six

Tucked against King, safe and warm, I couldn't see past the three other men other than in glimpses. What I did see was that Spartan, brother number five, did not look as happy, or as interested in what was going on as the others.

"Why is he here if he's in such a piss-poor mood?" I tried to lean around to get a look at him, curious.

"Because he is your fifth, and the final, of your choices, assuming you get to him." King ran a finger through my hair, parting several strands and braiding it back from my face. I leaned into him and a sigh slid from me.

"Well, he doesn't have to be here if he doesn't want," I said.

"He does, lass," Celt looked back at me, his eyes sad. "He don't want to be here, but he do *have* to be here. It is the binding placed on us that we will stand together. The call to you is too strong, even for him."

I closed my eyes. "Spartan, go if you want. I'm more than happy to choose from your four brothers."

There was a snarl from across the room, and I snapped my eyes open in time to see Preacher and Wick fly through the air. Celt was right behind them, shoved aside by a rather furious vampire coming straight for me.

Fear slid from me, and anger replaced it in rapid form.

A bully he was then? I'd dealt with bullies before and I was going to have none of it. I yanked myself away from King and stood on the bed with nothing but my still-damp pajamas on, as Spartan leapt to the edge. I pointed a finger at him, furious that he would hurt his brothers because of something neither he nor I, nor any of them, obviously had any control over. He pulled a sword from his side and swung it too wide.

King growled behind me. "Spartan, this is not the way."

I glared at Spartan. "Stop being an idiot, right now. I have no more say in this than you do, you fool." I glared down at him and he glared right back.

His burnished gold eyes narrowed further until they were merely slits.

If I'd thought King had jaguar eyes, I corrected myself. Spartan's golden eyes reminded me of nothing more than a large cat, a predator in every sense of the word. From his eyes to the wild tangle of dirty blond hair hanging over his face, obscuring his features, to the sword in his hand and the well-used armor on his chest and around his waist...all of it screamed warrior.

I refused to feel anything for this tit of a man. "You think you can just be a bully? Totally unacceptable. You don't have to like me, that's fine. I realize I'm not every man's cup of tea, but beating up on your brothers is stupid and unnecessary. What is wrong with you?"

He didn't lower his sword but his glare eased. "Why would you care what happens to them?"

The depth of his voice did very bad things to me, curling through me right to my center, and I had to clamp my knees together to remain standing, as undignified as it was. I clenched my jaw against the moan at the back of my throat.

From behind me, King shifted on the bed. "Spar, ease off. She's not like what we expected. She is nothing like the queen. She's...she's really quite lovely all around. I can see it already."

Spartan's eyes flicked to his brother, and I took the chance to look to Wick, Preacher, and Celt. The three of them watched with eyes the size of saucers.

Spartan slowly lowered his sword. "Fine. I will not kill her. But when it comes down to it, her life is forfeit over ours. I will not lose my brothers."

A shiver of fear sliced through me. "You think I'm not capable of standing up to that little twat of a girl out there?"

His eyebrows shot up. "Does she not frighten you?"

I frowned. "Does she frighten you?"

He nodded. "Yes. And if you were smart, you would be on your knees begging for your life right now."

A grin slid over my lips. "I'm sure I'll be on my knees later, but I doubt I'll be begging for my life."

Celt burst out laughing. "Oh, damn, lass. I do like ye better and better."

"Feeling's mutual." I gave him a rough salute as I stood on the bed, looking down at five very distinct, and all rather luscious, men. All of them mine, apparently.

Well, forgoing Spartan, which the more I looked at him, the more I'd like to see what he had under that armor. The tub would be a lovely addition, scrubbing his body down, letting the soap slick his body.

I cleared my throat and looked away.

"Okay. So, is there anything else I should know about this whole shindig? I've got six days to make a decision and then what?"

"Then you fight the queen," Spartan said. "You fight her and pray she kills you quickly."

I frowned. "I have to fight her?"

He snorted and turned away, the derision in his voice thick. "You can't fight, I take it?"

Without much thought, I leapt from the bed and landed on his back, wrapping my arms around his neck and pulling for all I was worth. I didn't really think I could hurt him. Not a vampire of his size.

But I caught him off guard as I squeezed with all my might. He scrambled at my legs while the other men hooted and hollered, and I rode him like a bucking bronco. He twisted and flipped me over his hips so he caught me in his arms.

His face was flushed. "If you are that eager to die, then do it now and do not bother with my brothers."

"Teach me to fight, then, if you're so damn smart!" I threw the words at him, a challenge and perhaps a plea for help. I could see he was indeed the fighter of the five. I needed all the help I could get if I had to fight for my life in less than a week.

He stared down at me, his fangs peeking past his lips, and I wanted nothing more than to suck on them, feel them drive into my neck...I shook myself. "I can control myself around you. Can you do the same long enough to teach me something that could save my life?"

"You can't learn to fight in five days. It's impossible," he snapped and let me go. I would have hit the floor if Celt hadn't caught me.

I smiled up at him. "Thanks, that could have left a nasty bruise on my bum."

"Ah, lass, I would have kissed it better."

I laughed and he helped me to my feet. I cleared my throat. "Spartan, will you help me? I am willing to believe in the impossible, especially now after all of this."

His shoulders hunched as if I'd hit him. "Damn your pull on me. Yes, I will teach you. During the day, you are mine to teach for at least four hours. The rest of the time..." He shook his head and flung a hand outward as if to encompass his four brothers. The rest of the time, I'd be bedding the men who wanted me.

Every part of me tingled in anticipation and I had to fight not to clamp my knees together and groan out loud.

"It's a deal then."

He grunted and stormed from the room, the pull between us not lessening but tightening like an elastic band. He wouldn't go far. I knew that as well as I knew my own mind. Whatever bond was between us would not allow him to leave me. At least, not until I was good and dead, I supposed.

"Do not think like that," Preacher said. "He will be a good teacher. It is a good compromise for him."

I glanced at Preacher and held a hand out to him. He drew close, took my hand and lifted it to his lips. Time for me to spill the beans to all of them.

"I...I've been cheated on before and I know how shitty it feels. I don't want you to feel like that, even while I can feel a pull to the others."

He smiled and shook his head. "There are no hard feelings, Allianna. You were brought to us, and were meant to be with us all. There will be a draw to us like nothing you've ever felt."

I looked at each of them. "So none of you mind? That I'll be with all of you?"

One by one they shook their heads, all with a smile on their lips. I clung to Preacher. "Are they telling the truth?"

Laughter filled the room. "Yes. They are. Allianna, you are doing nothing wrong. We want you, and you want us. There is nothing about that you should feel bad about."

I drew a slow breath and nodded once more.

"Is there anything else you should be telling me? I feel like you are holding back on the details of this."

The four men exchanged glances that were far more telling than if one of them had just said no, there was nothing left to say.

"Spit it out," I said. "Just rip the Band-Aid off. This is far more painful with the slow looks and—"

"You will choose one of us as your mate, and the other four will be sentenced to death," Preacher said.

I took a moment to make sure I'd heard right. My heart cranked up at a speed that had nothing to do with lust but pure fear for these men I'd only known such a short time. "Why?"

"It is an old rule from a long time ago," King said. "A time when a male harem was unacceptable, and the ruler was a male with a single queen. She was not to be touched by more than that one she was bound to."

I crossed my arms over my chest. "So, you mean to tell me you won't just drop dead. That someone would actually have to kill you?"

"Yes," Celt nodded. "That is correct, lass."

"And you wouldn't fight for your lives?"

The four shook their heads in unison. "No, we would not. Perhaps Spartan would," Wick said, his dark eyes on mine. "The truth is that the only way would be for you to be queen. Then you could change the rule and potentially save us. If that is your choice. It could be seen as weakness, which is why it has never been done before."

I drew a breath. My whole life I'd been writing, dreaming about a world I would fit in. Where the monsters and magic were real and the love was as intense as I'd always written. I looked from face to face of the four men in front of me. I knew that by saying what I was going to say, I was changing my life forever. There would be no going back to my home, to my sister Dominique, to my dog Luke. There would be no finishing that damn novel.

But I already knew that for these men, I would do it all. I would fight for them, like I'd never even bothered to fight for poop-face Mike.

Preacher snorted. "Poop face? That's what you call your ex?"

"Well, he's an ex for a reason," I pointed out with a slow smile that slid from my face faster than it grew. "We're in this together, then. All five of us."

Celt tipped his head to one side. "Six, if you want to count the child in the group."

From the room next to us, the wall shuddered as if someone had punched it. I lifted an eyebrow. "Spartan?"

The four of them nodded, once more in unison. I sighed. "Six then, against all odds."

Preacher was the first to come to me. He bent his head and kissed me gently, his lips tasting faintly of my own desire. I swallowed hard as he stepped back. King was next, and he lifted me so he didn't have to bend down.

His kiss was not as demanding as I would have expected from such a big man, his mouth tender and sweet and full of hidden promises. I couldn't resist. I flicked the tip of my tongue down the length of one fang.

He dropped me and backed away as the front of his pants tented. "Ah, you will have me tearing your clothes off, lady mine."

I shrugged. "We all have talents. I supposed that's mine?"

He followed Preacher to the door, a smile on his lips as he backed out. "Perhaps, it is."

Celt took my face in his hands. "Lass, you be coming to me at the end, I hope you're ready for me." He leaned in and took my earlobe in his mouth, sucking it, laving it as if it were my clit and not my ear. Fuck, just my ear in his mouth and I was writhing against him.

He let me go as suddenly as he'd taken hold of me, and then he, King and Preacher were gone, out the door.

Leaving me with Wick.

A low laugh rumbled from him as I slowly turned to face him.

I couldn't help the laugh that burst out of me when I saw him. He was completely naked and stretched out on the floor in front of the fireplace, his cock already at full attention, just waiting on me.

"In a hurry, are we?" I couldn't help the smile despite the dire odds against us, despite all the things I'd just learned. I just couldn't believe we wouldn't succeed. In my books, the underdog always won.

I was the underdog, so I had to win. There was no other answer I would allow myself to consider.

Wick winked at me, and crooked a finger. "Will you let me fuck you, Allianna?"

"Not the most romantic way of putting it, Wick." I took a step toward him as I lifted my shirt over my head. "But yes, I will fuck you. Only if you want it, though."

He made a motion at the lower half of his body. "Little hard to hide that I want you."

"Just being clear that we are on the same page." I shimmied out of my pants and kicked them behind me.

Another time, another place in my life I would have balked at this wanton behavior, I would have chastised myself severely. But I just couldn't. Not here, not now with this man whose laughter echoed my own.

I went to my knees beside him and arched an eyebrow. Waiting for him to make the move. For sure, I'd given consent, but I still wanted him to make the first move. To show me that he wanted me.

I didn't have to wait long.

Chapter Seven

Wick's body was as lean and hard as I'd imagined, perhaps even harder. There didn't seem to be an ounce of fat on him, showing every angle of his cut muscles. Yet, there was not a lot of bulk to him; these were the muscles of long years of hard work that had kept him trim.

He took both my hands and tugged me toward him, rolling me under his body so my back was pressed into the thick fur rug in front of the fireplace in my room.

"Were you a fighter, like Spartan?" I reached up and ran a hand over the side of his face, finding a faint pale scar that I traced all the way to his ear.

His lips quirked. "You like to talk during?"

"Before. During. After. Indulge me. I have to get to know you each over the next few days and decide which one of you is the man of my dreams." I waggled my eyebrows at him.

He flicked his tongue out the side of his mouth as if he were thinking. "I was a fighter, but as a slave, not a paid warrior like Spartan."

I narrowed my eyes, thinking. "If I were to put you in a book, I'd make you a thief. Lean, fast, with a sense of humor as sharp as a blade."

He threw back his head and laughed, exposing his throat and drawing me forward at the same time. I used his momentum to roll him so I was on top and he carried my weight. Both of his hands went to my ass, squeezing the twin globes. "Allianna, you are a very good guesser. I was a thief, after I broke free of my slaver. That is where I was found and brought before the queen."

I couldn't help the chuckle. "You were trying to steal from the vampire hive?"

He rolled his shoulders. "To be fair, I didn't know what they were, only that there were rumors of great wealth hidden deep in the hills of New England. That is manna and temptation together for a thief."

I lowered my face and began to kiss my way across his chest, finding the pale scars that marked him as a slave what I hoped was a long time past. "Talk to me, while I taste you," I said softly.

He sucked in a breath. "I thought I would be the one doing the work."

"You might be, but let me play." I nipped at his side, over his ribs, making him jump.

I looked up from under my lashes, and his dark eyes, they closed. "God, you will be the death of me. I know it. Already I would cast my life for yours, Allianna. Not since my maker has anyone ever commanded that from me."

My lips traced the curves and hard edges of his stomach, to the lines that pointed at the all but vibrating hard cock that waited for my touch.

"I was an orphan," he said, and I kissed the juncture of his hip and thigh, pressing his leg to one side.

"Oh, fuck, I won't last," he whispered.

I smiled and rubbed my face against his inner thigh, breathing in his smell of clean skin, dark nights, and the haze of a lightning bolt cutting through the air. Ozone seemed to trickle around us as I kissed and licked my way down to the back of his knee and back up again. "Talk to me, Wick."

"After I was captured and turned by the queen, I was sent out to recruit new members. It was my choice if they were worthy. I found King and Celt and knew they would fit well with Preacher and me. We needed more added to be a brotherhood. Spartan, on the other hand, he was brought in by one of the other brotherhoods, a violent group who like to abuse their women. But he wasn't going to fit with them. I knew it right away, so I stole him and brought him to Lily to turn for our brotherhood and now, if you don't mind, I think I've had enough of your brand of torture." The words had come out in a flying rush and he moved as if to sit up.

I leaned in and licked the base of his cock, stilling his movement as quickly as if I'd literally frozen him.

"You sure about that? You want me to stop?"

He lowered himself back. "Killing me, I tell you."

I licked up the base of his cock like a lollipop, curled my tongue around the tip and then trailed it back down. "Don't worry. I'd like you to return the favor at some point."

He buried his hands into the fur of the rug, unable to reach me where I sat between his knees. I slid my hand to either side of his cock and leaned over him, slipping the satin sheath of him in until the tip reached the back of my throat. I slid it out again, and in, over and over, tightening my lips here and there, swirling my tongue over him. Tasting him. Feeling my own pussy grow wet with wanting him even as I drew him closer to a climax. Feeling the heat between us growing and swirling like flames kissing against my skin. I groaned, and he arched into my mouth.

Shifting my weight, I moved so I sat to the side of him, well within reach of one of his hands. He took the unspoken offer, and worked his way up my inner thigh to the wet warm center of my body.

"Damn it, woman. I'm going to come."

I pulled my mouth off him and looked up his body. "You say that like it's a bad thing."

"One climax each, then you have to be passed on to the next. If you reach the last of us, and there is still time, you will start back at the beginning with Preacher."

His words echoed in my mind. Over and over, I would be shared among them.

Like a carousel of orgasms. A part of me wanted to squeal and jump up and down. If this was going to be the last week of my life, at least I was going out with a goddamn fucking bang-a-rama.

A tremble whispered over my limbs. "And I don't have to sleep?"

"And that drink will give you stamina to keep up with us," his finger dipped into me and did a slow circle, pressing outward. His thumb followed, pressing in deeply, and then he spread finger and thumb, stretching me ever so much that I forgot what I was doing, but instead stayed where I was and let the tug and pull on my pussy guide my movements.

"So that each of us can prove our worth to you, to prove we are the one that best fits your needs and wants." Wick twisted his hand half a turn and then back again as he began to pulse his hand slowly in and out of me. I was on my hands and knees, head down as I breathed through the pleasure as it built and grew, as the heat in my middle spread outward and my wanton hips rocked with him.

"I can bring you as many times as I want, but as soon as I come, I have to give you over to King," Wick said. "Which makes me want to fuck you, oh, so badly, but also, I want to hear you scream."

I was shaking and barely able to hold myself up, my pussy was dripping and I panted with need. Wick shifted so he still had his fingers in me, but also so his free hand was on one of my hanging breasts. He pinched a nipple, drawing it down and with that drawing a deep moan from me as the two pleasure centers collided in my belly.

"Do you want me to stop?" He whispered, "Just say the word and I will. I won't—"

"Don't you dare stop." I managed to speak around the growing struggle to breathe normally. A week of this and my heart was going to burst from sheer overload.

"Good." He slid under me and latched onto my other breast. His mouth and teeth suckled hard, drawing the nipple and my breast deep into his mouth as his finger and thumb spread and pressed my pussy wide.

"No fisting," I bit the words out, suddenly aware I needed to set some boundaries.

"M'kay," he said around a mouthful of tit. I wanted to laugh, but struggled not to. Maybe at some point I'd let him go further, but not tonight. Today, this morning. Hell, I had no idea what time it was. His thumb slid from my wet pussy and he slid in another finger.

At first, I didn't understand, and then his thumb circled up around my clit, wet with my own juices while his other fingers worked their magic inside me, stroking and pushing hard.

My hips began to work in time with his hand, slow and steady.

"Wick, please, I want you inside me." I whispered the words and the answering groan was all I heard as he unlatched from my breast and slid up so his face was right under mine. "A kiss then, and I'll do as you ask."

I was happy to oblige. I sat back on my knees and drew him with me so we were both on the rug, facing each other, arms wrapped around one another. His mouth tasted like the whiskey and I lifted an eyebrow. He winked. So, he'd snuck some of my whiskey, had he?

I bit his lower lip. "Bad, bad Wick. You're going to get a beating for stealing my drink."

His eyebrows raised and I wanted to smack my forehead. He'd been a slave; what was I thinking?

But his wide eyes were all mock innocence. "You can prove nothing."

I leaned in and kissed him again, deep, tasting every inch of his mouth. I pulled back only a little. "Sorry, evidence is there."

"Unless I beat you first?" he quipped as he spun me around so my back was to him and pushed me so I was back on my hands and knees. He bit my left ass cheek so suddenly I cried out, with pleasure, pain, and sheer surprise.

He chuckled. I threw a mock glare over my shoulder and he rubbed his face against my lower back. "Too hard?"

"No, I like a good bite," I said. He moaned something about temptation being too strong and how he'd like to sink his teeth into me.

His hands curled around and under me as he pressed himself between my cheeks, sliding his cock down over my tight ass bud to the wetness waiting on the other side. Back and forth, he slid so my moisture was everywhere. No matter where he placed his tip, I was wet. I pushed backward, a clear invitation to get him inside me. He took it, and pressed the tip of his cock into the edge of my pussy. I reached under and guided him in so he didn't slip out. Leaning on one hand as I was, I could reach back and stroke his balls with each thrust of his hips. A hiss slid from his lips.

"Allianna, stop, I will not last," he begged.

I dropped my hand, settling on the motion of our bodies rocking together, the feeling of his lower abs against my ass cheeks and the growing connection between us. He leaned forward and pressed his cheek against my back.

"Preacher warned me," he said. "But I did not believe him."

A groan slid from me as his fingers found my clit and rubbed a hard thumb across it. I didn't know if I wanted to buck against his thumb or his cock, so caught between the two ecstatic levels of pressure that made me want to come right then.

"He warned me that you would consume me, that your heart was bigger than even you knew. He can see all of you, and he was right. He knew the others would fail." He rocked against me harder and then softer, back and forth between tender and demanding as his thumb flicked and pressed in the same manner.

I whimpered, "Please, Wick, I'm so close. I want to come."

He sucked in a sharp breath, like he was gasping for each lungful. "Sweet girl, I can't hold off."

"Together then," I said, "come with me, Wick. Fuck me and don't stop."

He growled and the thrusting, the driving of his hard cock so deeply into me, the curl of the pleasure from his hands demanding that I rise with him were so intense, I had to close my eyes. I had to focus on my breath as the flesh of our bodies slapped harder and harder, as my hips rose to meet his and I couldn't stop. I didn't want to stop. Wick was mine, he was mine and there was an answer in his laughter that echoed my own, the same sense of humor, the same love of life.

I didn't want to stop. I wanted to ride this crest of pleasure with him over and over, and as I climaxed, screaming out for more, demanding he fuck me, I knew I would get a chance. I collapsed on the fur rug, burying my face in its softness and warmth, Wick on top of me, still inside me. He slowly kissed his way along my shoulders, to my neck, rolling me over so we faced each other.

His lips found mine and the leisurely way we pressed our mouths together, the way our tongues danced as if they'd known each other for years, all of it brought a strange feeling deep inside.

Love was not possible. I was no girl child to believe that, but I did recognize a kindred spirit in Wick. One left far too young to fend for itself.

"Your eyes are trying to speak to me," he murmured as he kissed the side of my mouth.

I ran my fingers down his back, knowing our time was drawing short.

"I'm an orphan too. I only have my sister."

His head drew up and he frowned down at me. "Why didn't you say that earlier?"

I shrugged. "I don't know, I just...I just know there is something between us I could not have imagined."

He brushed his fingers across the edge of my hairline. "More than Preacher?"

I frowned, thinking. "No, not more. Just...different."

He nodded, and kissed me with such tenderness that if you'd asked me even an hour before, I would have said he wasn't capable. That the laughing man would know nothing of sweet gentle lovemaking.

A knock at the door stilled his ministrations on my body. "Damn, I want more time, Allianna."

I smiled up at him, kissed him gently. "So do I."

He sat up, and helped me do the same. I took stock of my body, expecting there to be some tenderness from the two rounds of lovemaking and excessive orgasms of the day so far. As it was, though, I felt nothing but a sweet glow suffusing my limbs.

I drew in a breath. "That fire whiskey is something else."

Wick laughed and helped me stand. I stumbled and he caught me against his chest. Gently, so very gently, he kissed the top of my head. "Have fun with King, but not too much fun. I will have to find a way to outdo him when I see you next."

Laughter spilled up between us and he kissed me one last time before he gathered his clothes and left me there, naked and all alone.

I waited and when King did not immediately enter, I let out a breath of relief. Not that the thought of the green-eyed vampire didn't excite me, but to be honest, I wanted to wash a bit. The smell of Preacher and Wick clung to me, and while I didn't mind, I wanted to have a moment to freshen up.

That seemed only fair, to bed them each with a clean slate, as it were.

The shower was damn amazing. The second time, the water was the perfect temperature as I stepped under the rain head. I couldn't help but think of Preacher and his touch, the feel of his body on mine, which led to my first impression of Wick, which was so wrong. He was special, just not the same way Preacher was.

I scrubbed my body with the soap and lathered up my hair. I rinsed off, toweled off, and still there was no King to attend to me. Maybe I had to go find him? Maybe it was some sort of hide and seek that he wanted?

If that was the case, then I needed clothes. I circled the room to the tall wardrobe and peered into it.

Clothing of every color and style looked back at me, all of it women's clothes.

I pulled a few pieces out and held them up to my body. They looked like they'd been made for me. Which was impossible because no one had known I was going to be brought here. I frowned and pulled out more clothes, pulling tops on and off at random.

Every last piece was cut to my size.

Which had to mean someone had known I was coming, and they'd been waiting for me. I put a hand to the back of my head, thinking.

For the first time, I was alone without one of the men touching me and my mind was clear of the lusty haze that had so held me in its grasp.

There was no way that Spartan would be able to train me in five days to face that twat of a queen. No doubt she'd been training for this the last hundred years. My brain was finally back online after its trip to the orgasm house, and it was telling me it was not going to work long term. Dominique still needed me. Cassie still needed me.

"Shit, I've got to get out of here." I pulled the darkest clothes I could find out of the cupboard. A long dark sweeping skirt and a peasant blouse in the same shimmering black. I slid them on, the material ghosting over my skin and making me shiver.

I had to find the hospital area, get Cassie, and get us the hell out of here. Not only would that keep my life intact, but the brothers' too. If there were no potential queen to submit, then there was no reason to be killed, right? Seemed logical to me. I left, and no one would die. I nodded to myself, this was the right course of action. I knew it in my heart.

But why then did my heart cry out that I was losing something precious, just walking away from this world without even trying to fight for it?

Chapter Eight

I slipped out of my sumptuous room and into the hall-way. There were lights in the walls here and there. Not torches, but real electrical lights. So much for that fantasy; my bubble burst like a kid with a needle and a water balloon.

I kept to the far side of the hall and strode forward. Creeping would only intensify the image I was doing something I shouldn't be.

A man stepped from around a far corner. I made a beeline for him when I saw he was not one of the five brothers. "Excuse me."

He startled and stared at me as if I'd just spouted some sort of profanity at him. I smiled. "I'm looking for the hospital wing. Can you point me in the right direction?"

He continued to stare at me, his eyes wide.

My patience was not at an all-time high. I was going to run out of sand in the hourglass of my life if I did not make this happen right now. I snapped my fingers in front of his face. "Hospital wing, where is it?"

"T-t-t-that way." He pointed down the way he'd come. "D-d-d-down the set of stairs and stay to the l-l-l-l-eft."

I bobbed my head. "Thanks."

He pulled away from me as I went by like I had some sort of a virus and all but ran in the other direction.

I didn't care. I just wanted to get to Cassie. From there, I could get us both out of here, and the amazing, mind-blowing sex that I'd experienced would hold me over for years, maybe even decades. Because how could any human man possibly come close to bringing me that kind of pleasure? The men I'd been with in the past had either been rutting pigs, only worried about their own pleasure, or men who were so uncertain that they tried too hard, or wouldn't take direction because how could I, a woman, possibly know what felt good? None of those left me with anything but the need of a vibrator and the image of one of my heroes in my head in a large tub full of bubbles every Saturday night.

I sighed as I put my foot on the top step. A voice down the hall from where I'd come made me pause.

"What do you mean you don't know where she is? If the others get a hold of her, they'll kill her!" Wick's voice held a note of sheer terror.

Shit, someone else besides the queen might try and kill me? Those damn boys. They hadn't been honest, then. I frowned, doing what I could to harden myself against Wick's obvious worry.

Honesty was something I wanted, needed, after Mike's indiscretion. I shook my head and hurried down the stairs, moving as fast as I could without flat-out running. At the bottom, I stayed to the left, the hallway curling around and around until I came to a rather tiny door, not at all what I would have expected for a hospital. That should have been my first warning.

I pushed the door open and gagged on the smell floating out to me.

"Oh, my God, that is horrendous," I whispered through clenched teeth, going farther in, looking for any sign of a bed, or Cassie. I dared to call out for her, "Cassie?"

A low rumbling snarl stopped me in my tracks. The scent of dog mixed in with the smell of shit and rotting meat.

I bit my lower lip. "This isn't the hospital ward, is it?"

I don't know who I thought was going to answer me. There was the pulling sound of chains across the stone floor and then a massive, furred body flung toward me, claws outstretched.

I fell backward, scrambling on my ass to get back to the door. How far did the beast's chain stretch?

I pushed with all I had, fighting to get to safety. I refused to sit there and wait for someone to rescue me. The snapping teeth clashed shut right in front of my nose, and a big paw landed on the edge of my skirt, and pinned me to the floor.

The wolf was bigger than anything I'd ever seen, its body hulking and dark with shades of black and gray. The low rumbling growl echoing from its chest vibrated in my own. I held very still, knowing that any movement would send the beast over the edge. I'd seen the look in Luke's eyes more than once when he pinned a rabbit down. As long as the rabbit remained still, there was a chance it would be rescued. But if it moved...an image of white fur splattered with blood was all too strong and all too possible. Only, it would be my blood splattered on my black skirt and top.

If I was dealing with vampires, then this wolf might be no ordinary wolf. Just based on its size, I would guess it wasn't.

A werewolf, though, was part human, and therefore should have some capacity for understanding, shouldn't it?

"I don't know why you are here. But I can help you if you let me go." I whispered the words, afraid to so much as take a deep breath.

The growling deepened and the wolf took another half step, bringing its body over my own. I didn't lean back, which meant my face was pressed into the beast's shoulder. A distinct smell of clean air and deep summer nights whispered under the smell of death.

"You don't belong here," I said. "I'm so sorry."

I didn't know who I was apologizing to, but I felt it in my bones. This wolf was a prisoner, far more than I was. But that meant the two of us were really on the same side.

It sat down, and the growling stopped. My jaw dropped.

"You understand me?"

The deep brown eyes regarded me, and then slowly it nodded, the chain rattling slightly. I drew a breath as I shook my head. "They will probably kill me too, you know. Maybe I should just let you have at me."

A sharp grunt from the wolf and it shook its head. It made a motion as if to shoo me out of the room with one big floppy paw. I stood and stared down at it.

"If I survive, I'll free you. I promise."

The wolf lay down and watched me as I backed out of the room and quietly shut the door. Only then did I realize how close I had come to being bitten, eaten, or maybe worse, turned into a werewolf. I sank to the ground, my legs no longer able to hold me upright. Tears slipped down my cheeks, as much for the scare as for the beast behind the door. I had no doubt it was the queen who kept him there. I pushed to my feet, so angry I could have throttled her right there, if she'd been available for throttling, that was. I turned and headed back up the stairway as the sounds of running feet came hammering down.

I pressed myself against the side wall, thinking they would pass me by. But they turned out to be just one set of feet, and that one turned out to be Spartan.

He grabbed my arms and yanked me hard which flung me into his chest.

"Where the hell do you think you were going?"

I stared up at him, still flushed with fear from the beast, and embarrassingly my eyes welled up. I tried to jerk my arm away from him but he didn't let me go. Instead, he began to drag me up the stairs.

I didn't dig my heels in, but instead followed meekly behind. However, at the top of the stairs, I pulled back, putting enough weight into it that Spartan paused and looked back at me.

"Is there more danger than the queen?"

His jaw ticked and he nodded. "My brothers didn't want to tell you."

Now my jaw ticked. "They did lie to me, then."

"If you want to look at it that way, yes. What were you doing outside the room?" His gaze seemed to burn through me and I found myself looking away.

He snorted. "You want honesty, but don't want to give it. Typical."

I whipped a hand around and slapped his face so hard my hand smarted all the way up to my elbow.

"Don't you ever lump me into a group with faithless, brainless women."

His glare hardened and the exquisite lines of his mouth thinned. "Then what were you doing outside the room?"

"My friend is here somewhere. They said in a hospital. I asked a vampire I saw and he sent me—"

Spartan jerked me forward until we were nose to nose. "What did he look like?"

"What?" I found the intense proximity a bit much. I had a hand on his chest and was using it to balance myself, but if I just leaned in a little more, maybe our lips would touch.

No. The thought stopped me. Spartan hated me, and I would not fall to the lust curling through me.

"What did the vampire look like? He gave you directions to the chained wolf?" He blinked. "Did you go into the wolf's den?" Without waiting, he bent his head and drew in a deep breath from around me. "You went to the wolf and survived?" Those golden eyes were so round with shock that another time I would have laughed.

"She shouldn't have chained him up," I said. I closed my eyes, trying to think about what the other vampire had looked like.

"The vampire who gave me directions was taller than you, but soft, like he had no muscle. He stuttered when he spoke, but I assumed that was shock." I blinked up at Spartan. "Does that help?"

Spartan was staring at me, his eyes somewhat unfocussed. I lifted a hand and touched the side of his face, as carefully as I could. "Spartan, does that description help?"

With a shake of his head, he broke whatever spell he was under and at the same time pulled his face away from my hand. "Yes, it does. I'm taking you back to the room. King should be there now."

He started down the hall, his hand still firm on my arm, but no longer bruising. He glanced at me several times as we walked. Finally, I gave up.

"What? What is it you are looking for on me? I am not bruised or beaten up. Nothing is hurt more than my ego." I brushed his hand that held me and he let go. "I'm not running away. I wanted to see my friend." And then run away.

I think his lips twitched. "You can't read minds like Preacher, can you?"

Spartan's lips twisted a bit more. "No."

That made me like him more. Not that Preacher reading my mind was a bad thing, but it was also nice to have my thoughts to myself without filtering them first.

At the doorway to the room, he kept on walking, leaving me to watch him go. "Hate to see you leave, love to watch you go," I whispered to myself. Damn, he cut a nice figure. Bigger across the chest than the other men, he was truly built like a war machine. He paused at the intersection at the far end of the hall.

"I thought you wanted to see your friend. Are you coming with me or not?"

My jaw dropped, but I snapped my mouth closed in an instant and ran down the hall, scooping up the skirts so I could catch up to him.

"You'll take me to see her?"

"That's what I said, isn't it?" He frowned at me. "Are you so used to being lied to?"

I chuckled. "You have no idea."

He looked away and started down the hall. "I won't lie to you, Ally. I'll be a bastard. I may try and kill you, but I won't lie to you."

"Fair enough. And I won't try to draw you into my bed while I'm still alive."

That slowed his feet. "Then you admit, you're likely to die."

My shoulders slumped. "Yes. Five days of training even with the mighty Spartan won't change my fate, I think. And I doubt I'd be able to escape this place, even if I could hold my head above the raging hormones for more than a few minutes at a time."

He shook his head. "Is that what you were doing? Escaping?"

I could lie to him, but we'd both know it. "Sort of escaping? I wanted to find Cassie, and I...Spartan, I understand why you hate me. I get it. I represent death for either you and three of your brothers, or if I were to choose you to stand next to me, your four brothers would die. No partnership is worth that. I thought if I slipped away, you five would be okay, at least. I'd have some wild memories, and when one day I'm old and gray I will look back and say this was the moment I felt beautiful for the first time in my life."

He stopped, those eyes on me and I couldn't meet his gaze. Something tightened in my chest, an emotion I didn't want. A kind of grief knowing I only had days to live. That Spartan knew I only had days. I brushed a hand across my eyes. "As I've pointed out, I'm not a young girl. I know how the world works. It is not a fairy tale. There are rarely happily-ever-afters, no matter how bad we may want them."

I tried to give him a smile. I really tried, but I struggled to lift my lips. He brushed a loose wave of my hair behind one ear. "We'll get you in fighting shape. King can wait a little for his turn. I'll take you to see your friend, then to the training field. At least, you'll go down swinging."

I blinked up at him, knowing his words for what they were. Hope, and kindness, far more than I expected. I nodded slowly, taking his hand in mine and lowering it from my face. "Thank you." But the words neither of us spoke were far deadlier. He pulled his hand away from me, a little slower than before.

We both knew my life was forfeit. That he would try and help me survive at all told me the kind of man he was. The kind that I could always depend on, the kind that would never lie to me. Why the hell couldn't I have found these five brothers before now?

Because, Ally, this is the world of vampires and you never knew it existed before.

Right, there was that. I sighed and followed Spartan deeper into the vampire hive, trusting him with my life. Only when it was too late did I learn the foolishness of that choice.

Chapter Nine

Spartan led me through the hive, and I did my best to pay attention to the twists and turns, but there were two things against me. One, there were so *many* twists and turns that after the eighth, I couldn't recall what the third turn was, left or right or straight on through. The other was that Spartan was a few feet ahead of me, which gave me a lovely view of his legs and back. His ass was covered by the metal plating armor that seemed to have come right out of the movies and every Spartan character I'd ever seen. I liked it. Right down to the boots he had laced up to where they brushed his kneecaps.

The lines of his legs drew my eyes up, up over his ass and to the spread of his back. Easily, I caught glimpses of it here and there, the muscles moving effortlessly. There were also several tattoos from what I could see, though none of them clearly.

"What are your tattoos of?" My voice echoed strangely in the narrow hall.

He glanced over his shoulder. "I have four. Three on my back. They cover old wounds."

"And the fourth?" I noted he didn't answer my exact question.

"You'll never see the fourth." He said.

I bit my lower lip but then thought, screw it. "That sounds like a challenge if ever I heard one."

"No challenge. You won't ever see me in less than this. I need to be ready."

I arched both eyebrows, even though he had his back to me. "Ready for what?"

"If you are named queen, my brothers who are not chosen will bow their heads and allow themselves to be killed. It is a spell laid on them."

I snorted. "If by some unreal miracle I became queen, I would not allow it."

He snorted right back at me. "You cannot stop all the queen's guards. They will still work on her orders, even if you are named the heir. The queen's last wishes are always carried out after she dies."

I wondered what would happen if she was dead before the fight, but I smartly did not ask that question out loud. I suspected it might be trouble for me if I wandered around talking about killing the current queen. Even if she was a cunt.

Spartan came to a wider passage and took the left-hand turn. "We are almost there. If your friend is alive, she will be there."

I leapt forward and grabbed his arm. "Wait, what? What do you mean *if* she's alive?"

Spartan paused and let out a breath. "Malcom brought you in with his pack of idiots?"

"Ball-smashed Malcom, yes." I nodded. Spartan lifted his eyebrows.

"Ball-smashed?"

"I smashed his balls when he tried to tell me I had to suck them. It seemed an appropriate punishment."

Spartan leaned back and roared with laughter, full-bellied and echoing in the hallways. I put my hands over my lips, trying to stifle my own laughter, finally breaking and slapping my hands over his mouth. The feeling of his lips under my fingers was a temptation for sure, but I was mostly trying to get him to stop. For some reason, I had the feeling we would get in trouble if he was caught with me. If he was caught laughing with me.

"Shut up, someone is going to hear you. And you laugh like a damn dragon."

This only brought another peal out of him. I slapped him on the shoulder. "I mean it. Shut up."

"Oh, God. You crushed his balls! He was complaining about that, but he told us...he told us he got in a fight with a werewolf." He wiped a hand over his face as he finally caught a breath. "I would pay to see that. Maybe get it on video and watch it over and over."

Now it was my turn to snicker. "Stop. If I see him, and you're with me, I'll do my best to give you a repeat, okay?"

The smile on his lips faded as he put his hand on the door in front of us. "I'm sorry. I shouldn't have—"

"What, had a laugh? Dude, you can laugh. I'm good with laughter." I patted him on the arm, as if he were a friend. Maybe he didn't hate me as I'd first thought, but I did understand why he didn't want to like me. If it were the boys' lives against Dominique, of course, I'd choose my sister. I'd hate myself for doing it, but I would still do it.

He swung the door open and we stepped into a place that finally looked like a hospital. All white, bright lights, sterile smells and the soft murmur of voices that was as familiar to me as if I'd stepped back into the room where the doctors pronounced my parents' deaths.

Car accident. They'd died on impact.

But they weren't here, Cassie was. I could hear her laughter deeper in the room and I followed the sound. Around a white curtain, I found her flirting shamelessly with what looked to be her doctor. There was a thick bandage on her neck and she batted her long fake eyelashes over her bright green eyes up at the doctor. She didn't even see me at first, so wrapped up in his gaze as she was.

"You think maybe we can go for a drink after I get out of here?" She smoothed out the sheet over her legs with her hands, a nervous tic of hers.

The doctor patted her hand, and turned to see us. "We can talk about it," he said.

I saw the glimmer of his fangs as he spoke. Vampire doctor, that seemed a bit of an oxymoron. Cassie turned, following his gaze.

"O. M. G. Ally! What are you wearing, and who...is... that?" Her eyes widened as she stared past me at Spartan, no doubt.

"That's my bodyguard," I said. "I've been chosen for a high-stakes game of cat and mouse and he's got to keep me alive to the end. If I win, I become queen. If I lose, I lose my head."

She laughed and waved a hand at me. "Oh, please, you're so full of shit." She patted the bed and I went and sat beside her. I took her hands in mine.

"How are you feeling?"

She shrugged. "Okay, I guess. Doctor McDreamy there says I *have* to stay in for at least a week. That seems like a long time to me, but then I get to work on him taking me out to dinner." She sighed deeply. "Oh, how I'd like to work on him with some body lotion and a cock ring."

Spartan coughed. "I'll wait for you outside the hospital."

I glanced back in time to see him disappear around the curtain. I scooted up to the head of the bed and put my mouth next to Cassie's ear. "Do you understand that these are real vampires and that we are seriously deep in shit?"

"Yes." Our eyes locked and she nodded.

"Okay, stay quiet, try to gather a weapon or something. I'm going to get us both out of here." I glanced over my shoulder again.

"How?" Cassie whispered. "I'm so sorry. I don't even remember texting you."

"I'm not sure you did. I think they've been watching me for a while." That was the only thing that made sense with the perfect clothes. But was it the five brothers who'd been watching me or someone else? I'd put my money on someone else, but maybe that was just because I didn't want to believe the five men working their ways into my heart and body could be at fault.

"If...if I'm not back in six days, Cassie. You have to be ready to make a run for it, okay?" I wrapped my arms around her and a quiet cry slid from her lips.

"I don't want to leave without you. You're my best friend," she whispered.

"I don't want that either, but we may have no choice. I will do all I can on my side of things. You need to be ready on yours to leave with me, or, if you know a way out, you take it—"

She grabbed at my arm and pointed above our heads. I stared at the hole in the ceiling that was like an open chimney, all the way up to a skylight above. A thin shaft of sunlight glimmered down at us.

A skylight into the outside world.

I nodded. "Now, that, we can work with."

The ceiling was easily twelve feet, but once we were into the chimney, we could set our backs against one side and our feet on the other.

Hope flared. I could save the five men, and myself. I was sure of it. I just had to get out of their lives.

A pang around my heart had me rubbing at my chest, which I didn't like. I didn't love them, but damn if it wouldn't hurt to walk—or in this case—run from them.

I hugged Cassie tightly. "That's perfect."

"Well, I've been staring at it for the last day," she grumbled at me.

I blinked. "A whole day?"

"Far as I can tell." She nodded, her eye squinting with concern. "Why?"

My timeline was off. "Five days then, and you leave," I said softly. "Not six." I leaned over her and kissed her forehead. "Rest and gain your strength. And try not to molest Dr. McDreamy. I think he might have more bite in him than you realize."

We parted on laughter that hid the truth. We both knew we were in trouble, but then again, we'd been in trouble before and managed to get out.

That time in the canyon when the floodwaters came through.

Going to Vegas with nothing more than the clothes on our backs and a hundred dollars between us.

Breaking into her ex's apartment to steal info that helped her court case against his cheating ass.

I had to believe being here in the hive was no different.

A snort escaped me; even I had trouble believing that.

I wove my way through the hospital, taking note there was only one attendant besides McDreamy, and two other patients. Both of them chained to their beds by arms, legs and necks. The attendant saw me looking and pulled the curtains around the chained men quickly.

I looked away and let myself out into the narrow hall that was the hive. I couldn't help them for shit. I couldn't even help myself.

From one step to the next, the light around me changed. My eyes struggled to compensate going from a bright white hospital to the dark gothic nature of what almost felt like a castle straight out of a vampire movie. Underground, of course. Which made sense with the whole sunlight business.

Spartan leaned against the far wall opposite the hospital entrance.

"Nice visit?"

I tucked my hands behind my back. "I told her to try and get away if I didn't come back in five days."

He startled, then nodded. "Yes, she's being kept alive until after the Challenge is complete."

"And if I win?"

"She lives."

I shivered, cold with the realization of how many lives depended on me being able to face that scrawny twat of a queen. "You'll work with me now?"

"Don't you want to go to King?"

I swallowed hard. "Yes, but I think I would be able to enjoy my time knowing that I've done all I can to make myself ready."

Spartan said nothing, just turned down a new hall leading away from the hospital.

"Can you fill in a few things for me?" I asked.

He didn't look back, but he nodded. "If I can."

"Vampires don't like sunlight?"

"Correct. It won't kill us right away, but think of it as slowing us down to a human speed, and making us weak, easier to kill."

Made sense. "Garlic, crosses, fire?"

"We wound the same as if we were human," he did glance back then, "we can be killed by beheading, disembowelment, fire, crushed in a car accident, poison. But we heal faster, so unless the wounds are truly mortal, we could come back with some fresh blood."

"On that note," I said, "why didn't Preacher or Wick bite me?"

Spartan paused and I almost caught up to him before he started off again. "They won't bite you."

I frowned. "Won't, or aren't allowed?"

"You will choose your mate. He will bite you sealing the bond between you."

I followed him quietly after that, thinking through what he'd told me. A few minutes later the hallway opened into a large, cavernous room with a domed ceiling. "It makes me think of the Colosseum." I did a slow turn, checking the place out.

"Patterned after it in a fashion. Easier to train with a great deal of room."

There were no other trainees in the large area that spanned the size of a football field. Big indeed.

Spartan led me to the middle of the space. "It will all be hand to hand when you fight Terra, no weapons."

"Well, that's a start," I said. "Wait, Terra is her name?"

Spartan tipped his head. "It is."

"Terra the Twat." I punched one hand into my open palm of the other. "Fitting."

Spartan fought a smile. I could see it on his lips trying to ease across his face, but he managed to get rid of it.

He didn't answer, which didn't make me feel all that much better. "Hold your hands up, as if you were going to punch me."

I fisted my hands and brought them up, angling my stance. A few karate classes would at least help me not look like a complete tool when it came to the starting point.

His burnished gold eyes swept over me while he slowly circled around to the back side of me. I held my place, waiting for instruction, trying not to think about my vulnerability to him.

"Is it okay? How I'm standing?"

"Hard to say. I can't see your legs." He dropped to one knee beside me and pulled a knife from his belt. Before I could so much a launch a formal protest, he grabbed a handful of my skirt and slashed off enough that the new and raggedy hem kissed me at mid-thigh.

The air on my bare legs was refreshing, but I was also intensely aware of Spartan's hands on my skin as he adjusted my stance. He gripped my lower thigh, his hands big enough to wrap almost all the way around. "A bit wider there. And bend at the knee. Yes, like that."

From there on out, he didn't touch me, and my awareness of him changed. While I was still feeling his every move, the focus on fighting helped to keep the burning hormones at bay.

For what was at least two hours we worked on my defenses, on what to watch for when the queen came at me, at how to take a blow, how to strike with as much power as I could at the perfect moment.

Of all that, learning to take a hit was the hardest of the lessons in the most literal of senses.

We were sparring, and Spartan swung an open-handed blow aimed for my head. I thought I could block it in time and swept both my arms up, crossed at the wrists. I did manage to block his hand, but I had no way to stop all that power behind it. Which meant my own arms and crossed wrists were slammed into my head with the force of Spartan's muscles behind them.

I went down, flat out on my back, and found myself blinking up at the ceiling as the world danced and tumbled around me.

Spartan was there in a flash, kneeling beside me, his hands on either side of my head. "Shit, are you okay? Talk to me, Ally, talk to me."

"I'm seeing stars, and a large vampire with golden eyes. I must be dead, right?"

He closed his eyes. "Shit, don't do that to me. I thought I hurt you."

I carefully pushed to a sitting position. "Well, I'm not going to lie and tell you that it felt good, but I think I'll be okay."

"That's enough for today. The others—they would not forgive me if something happened to you while you were in my care." His words were...careful. Like he was speaking to himself as much as to me.

He stood but didn't hold his hand out to me. I understood. The less we touched, the easier it was to deny the pull between us.

I dusted off what was left of my skirt. "Same time tomorrow?"

"Every second fuck." He said the words as monotone as I think was inhumanly possible.

"After Celt, then?"

"Yes. You have to have time with them, and one of them must stand with you."

I took a step, testing my legs. No wobbling, so that was good. "What is that all about exactly? I mean, the bare minimum was explained to me, and I suspect there is more."

"I can't tell you." We had walked the length of the open training field and were back to the narrow hallways.

"You *can't* tell me, or you won't?"

"That is not a lie, but a rule. If I could tell you I would." He shook his head. "But I can't. Please do not ask it of me."

Damn, I only wanted to know more now. A mystery wrapped in a conundrum was this place and the men who'd come into my life.

It seemed like a very short time before he was dropping me off at the room. My room, to be exact, in the center of a hub. The five brothers were housed around the same hallway, close enough that they could be there for their time with me.

A thought rolled through me, what I would say was my writer's mind doing what it did best. Causing trouble and offering possibilities I didn't truly want to consider.

I bit my lower lip. "King knocked on the door, Spartan. He knocked but then he wasn't there. That's why I was able to get all the way down the stairs."

Spartan paused. "It wasn't him. I trust my brothers with my life, and I know King. He might come off as aloof from time to time, but I guarantee he would not put your life in danger."

I didn't want to point out that that seemed to be Spartan's job, as it were, at least according to my first impressions with the whole sword bit. Then again, other than that moment, he'd behaved admirably. More than I would have expected just a day ago.

A day already, how was that possible? Maybe time ran differently here, twisting and turning as much as the hive tunnels did. Anything was possible, I supposed.

"Thank you, for training me," I said. "I'll do my best to smash Malcom's balls for you before I go."

His eyebrows shot up. "That's a nice way of saying before you die."

"Don't remind me." I pushed him gently, the flat of my hand on his chest. I turned to the door and let myself in. I leaned against the door once it was closed, my eyes shut tightly. For just a moment, I wanted to let myself believe Spartan would be in the room with me, touching and teasing me, laughing and relishing the heat of our combined bodies. I knew it was not to be, but that didn't mean I couldn't dream.

Chapter Ten

"What thoughts roll beneath those sea-blue eyes of yours, princess?" King's voice tumbled to me, and my eyes opened. The room was transformed from what it had been.

The sheets changed from the dark blue to a deep red covered in white rose petals. Around the edges of the bed was a multitude of tall candles that gave off a flickering light, as if beckoning me forward.

King stood next to the bed, surprisingly with clothes on. The same cream-colored loose pants as before, bare-chested, though, and that was still a nice image. All that worked to steal my better judgment from me, and I squared my shoulders and clung to the handle of the door. If I had to run, I would.

I needed to be ready if I didn't like his answer.

"Did you hear me question Spartan?" I needed to clear the air. I would not sleep with a man I suspected had set me up to be killed. No matter how stunning he was to look at.

He bowed his head, that auburn-kissed hair falling forward. "Yes, I heard your questions to him."

"Were you not supposed to come for me next after Wick?" I couldn't help the sharp tone. These men I barely knew, yet found myself caring for, I was trying to save them. The least they could do was understand my life was in danger. Which reminded me that not all the information had been given to me.

"And since when does *not* telling me about all the dangers count as honesty? If anyone had bothered to tell me I was in danger not just from the queen but from other vampires, I might have stayed in the room." The words were hot, and he kept his head bowed. I knew it wasn't truly fair to chastise him like this. It wasn't just his fault I hadn't been told all the truth and nothing but the truth. But he was here, and the others were not. Which meant he was getting the short end of my temper.

His head was still lowered as he spoke. "Allianna, I am sorry. I was preparing things to make this special. I should have been here."

"And I was almost killed for it," I said.

His head snapped up and his nostrils flared. "What?"

"I left the room, and I took the advice of another vampire, directions to the hospital to see my friend. And instead, I ended up in the room with a giant werewolf that almost killed me." A shudder ran through me. "I just want you to be honest. If you don't want to be here with me, then go. I do not want more lies in my life. I won't have it."

I closed my eyes, a growing surge of emotion swelling in me. The wolf. Cassie in the hospital with the bandages on her neck. Fighting with Spartan. Realizing that I was going to die at the hands of the bitch queen Terra.

I burst into ugly, fear-filled tears, unable to contain them any longer.

"Allianna," the words sounded as if they pained him, "there is so much we are forbidden to tell you. I...I want to be here with you, and I swear it on my life that I will protect you. I will keep you safe even if it means my own death."

"I don't want you to die." I sobbed the words. "I don't want any of you to die."

In seconds, King scooped me into his arms and carried me to the bed. I curled against his chest, sobbing my heart out. I wrapped my arms around his neck and clung to him, to his solid warmth and the sudden certainty that he would do all he could to protect me.

That certainty spread, and I knew Spartan was right about King and his other brothers. They would not fail me. If anyone would fail, it would be me when I faced Terra, and it would cost them their lives. That thought sent off a whole fresh onslaught of tears. All of which King patiently and gently wiped away while he held me tightly against his chest, never once trying to stop me from crying.

The tears ebbed, a final hiccupping sob rolling from me. "I'm sorry. I think you have a fair number of tears and far too much snot on your perfect chest."

"Perfect chest?"

I loosened my hold on him, and looked up into his face, searching for a hint of duplicity there. But in those green eyes I saw nothing but a faint sadness, and I knew I'd caused it. "I am so sorry. I shouldn't have yelled at you."

He smiled and shrugged. "I am a strong enough man to carry a few of your tears on my most perfect chest."

A knot that had tightened in my chest slowly eased. "Thank you."

He stood, lifting me with an ease that sent a little thrill through me. "Let's get you cleaned off. You have dirt on your knees and elbows from your training."

The sway of his steps lulled me, even in that short distance from the bed to the spa bathroom. The candles were halfway burned down, but still gave a flickering glow to the room, like a dream. Like once more, this wasn't real. I let that belief stick with me, feeling safer in my dream world.

King set me on the tile floor, flicked on the shower heads and proceeded to peel my sweat-stained, chopped-up skirt and top from my body. I moved to touch him, to slide my fingers into the top of his pants, and he shifted out of reach.

My heart sank. He didn't want me, like Spartan. Funny how only a short time ago I wasn't sure I wanted him, and now being denied, my feelings were hurt. I pulled my shit together.

"I'm sorry. I shouldn't have assumed." I headed to the shower, but his hand on my arm stopped me.

"I do want you, Allianna. But according to my brothers the heat rises fast between you and your partner, and I want this to last as long as it can." He made a motion to the shower. "In with you."

A careful smile crept across my lips. Mostly because I was trying not to gleefully grin that King still wanted to bed me. I stepped into the shower and a moment later his hands were there, lathered in soap.

"Arms up," he said, his voice brooking no argument. Obediently, I put my arms over my head, facing him while the water streamed against my back. He started at my fingertips, working the soap over my skin, inch by inch, all the way down my arms to my shoulders. Almost professionally, he washed over my breasts, and belly, into the hollow of my belly, my hips, thighs and calves. Cherished, he made me feel cherished in a different way than the others. And like the others, he seemed to have no problem with the fact that he was sharing me with three other men. Perhaps my fears were ungrounded after all. Perhaps I could have my hot man cakes and eat them too.

"Turn," he said, "the rest of you is dirty too."

A laugh escaped me as I did as he asked. My face and chest were hit with a heavy stream of water, and King's hands began to work a wicked magic on my back. I lowered my hands and pressed them against the wall as the strength of his hands bled through to me. He massaged my muscles as though he knew exactly where they were stiffening. He worked down my spine and into the hollow of my back, taking great care. Over my buttocks, taking extra time with each cheek before sliding down the backs of my thighs, over my calves, and then went so far as to pick up each of my feet in turn, washing the bottom. He swept back to my ass, his hands gliding over my skin, circling around, higher and higher until he was at the top of my cheeks, caressing now more than massaging.

"That won't get any dirt off." I peeked at him from under the stream of water. A grin quirked his lips to one side.

"True enough. But I'm hardly done." He used his thumbs, working them in deep swirls that pressed into my flesh, lifting each cheek, spreading them ever so slightly as he slid down farther, to the tops of my legs, all the way to the back of my knees, my calves, and then back up.

"Turn."

I was shivering with a growing want; the slow build of touch and heat grew with each passing second under his fingertips as he drew lines over my skin. Designs of desire. This time, King slid his hands over my shoulders and around my breasts, far slower this time, swirling the soap, slicking my skin and making my body a veritable slippery-slide playground.

"Can I touch you?" I couldn't help the way my voice sounded all breathy, and to be honest, I didn't care.

"Not yet." His breathing was not much more even than mine as he slid his hands down my belly, skimmed my hips and slid around my inner thighs. His hand was slick as he moved the palm over my clit and pussy, and the flat pressure drew a groan from my lips. He pulled his hand back up, letting his fingers trail through my folds, up to my belly button.

"King?"

"Yes?"

"I really, really want to take this further."

He grinned at me. "Yes, we'll get there, oh impatient one."

His hands, the deep flexing of his fingers into my overworked muscles relaxed me in a way I didn't know I needed.

"On the bench." He gave the direction with the air of not often being told no. Here was the arrogance I'd have expected of a man named King.

I lifted my hands over my head and let the water sluice off my skin, removing the last of the soap. Because I was hoping I was right about what was going to happen.

God, I hoped I was right.

I moved to the bench and sat with my knees clamped together. Behind me a stream of water slid from an opening above our heads, like a waterfall that cascaded down to the bench. Warm water slid around me, tickling the edges of my body.

King stepped into the shower, his cock outlined against his loose wet pants. Big, big boy, bigger than either Wick or Preacher.

I licked my lips as I stared at him, wanting all of him in me, every last inch. He groaned.

"Do not look at me like you want to—"

"Eat you?" I supplied the words and smiled up at him, slowly crossing my legs. With my already slick skin it became a deliciously sexy move. "Don't you want to be...eaten? I do."

His eyebrows shot to his hairline and then just as quickly narrowed. "Is that a request?"

I shrugged one shoulder, trying to play it cool, which was a bit silly considering I was sitting there naked, waiting for the word to throw my legs open wide for him. "A demand might be a more accurate word."

He dropped to his knees in front of me and put a hand on either knee, slowly pushing my legs apart. With a tug, he brought my bottom to the edge of the seat. It was only then I realized that the bench was a perfect height for exactly this. For a woman being pleasured by a man.

He held my legs apart and lowered his face to the inside of one knee. He sucked at the skin, making a soft popping noise, he pulled at it so hard. I squirmed in my seat, wanting that pressure on my pussy and clit, not the inside of my knee. With great care and attention, he worked his way up the inside of my leg until his mouth hovered over my folds.

His breath tickled at my skin. "No hair."

"Waxing," I whispered, unable to take my eyes from the top of his head. King looked up at me and grinned.

"Lovely, so lovely to see all of you unhidden from my gaze." He flicked the tip of his tongue out and teased the folds, brushing against my clit. I whimpered and tried to push closer, but he held me in place with his hands on my knees.

The water licked at my back and King slowly licked at my front, parting my folds with stroke after stroke, using the tip of his tongue and then the flat. He put his entire mouth over my pussy and drove his tongue inside me, catching me off guard.

I arched against him, finding handholds on either side of the bench to help me steady my body. "Yes, please, yes." The words were a whispered plea. The sound of the water around us, the feel of his tongue, all of it bringing me to a crest. Already? Or was I just getting better at finding my orgasm?

He pulled back from my pussy and looked up at me. "You taste like heaven, Allianna. I want to taste all of you."

I swallowed with some difficulty around the sudden dry mouth I had. "Yes. I want that too."

King carefully tugged me forward so my legs were around his upper chest and then he *stood up.*

I let out a squeaking eek as he carried me out of the bathroom, his face between my breasts. He didn't let a moment go to waste as he caught the underside of one breast in his mouth, sucking on it the way he'd done the inside of my knee, making the skin suction tight before releasing it, drawing the blood to the site, leaving a mark on me that was his own.

We reached the bed and he lowered me, shoulders first so my legs were still wrapped around his chest. He gave me a deliciously naughty grin. "This is convenient, don't you think?"

His mouth descended on my pussy, and I could do nothing but writhe under his care. I cried out as the heat from his mouth, the flick of his tongue over and over my clit, harder and faster, brought that slow build of luscious pressure low in my belly, that pressure that meant I was coming hard and fast.

Right before I reached the crest, he pulled his mouth away and I cried out from the sheer loss. I squirmed where I was as the sensations faded. "That's not fair."

"You'll thank me later." He let my legs drop and slid between them, lowering himself on top of me. The bed sank only a little under our combined weight. The smell of the rose petals and the sweet soap he'd used on my body floated around us. My skin was still wet from the shower, and my pussy was wet with need.

But I wanted more than just the sex, and I knew it now. I wanted to know who these men were who put their lives on the line for me. Who would die if I failed, and did so willingly.

"Why King? Why that name?"

He pressed his mouth against the hollow of my throat and kissed his way up to my mouth. "I don't want to discuss it."

I sighed as his mouth traced patterns across my face, so gentle, so careful, as if I were the most precious thing he'd ever held. He wasn't even giving me his full weight, I knew because the press of his cock still was held back by the thin material of his pants.

"I don't want any of you to die for me." The words came out suddenly. He paused in his ministrations and looked down at me.

"That is our choice."

"It's unfair, and I won't have it." I ran a hand through his thick hair. "I'm not a fool. I know this isn't love. But that doesn't mean I don't care. Nor does it mean I would throw away any of you."

"Not even me?"

I frowned at him. "Why would I throw you away?"

"Because you believed I set you up to die."

I closed my eyes. "That was a mistake. Did you not believe my apology?"

He closed his eyes but not before I saw the flash of pain. I put both hands on his face. "King, look at me."

He opened his eyes and I held him so he could not look away. "I am sorry, but I've been hurt by men enough times to shoot first and ask questions later, as the saying goes. I was wrong. I trust you. I trust Spartan. I trust Preacher and Wick and even Celt. Trust is not something I normally give this easily, but it feels like you all have a part of my soul that I had no idea was even missing."

He pressed his forehead against mine. "I was a slave. For many years before Lily became my queen and I rose out of the filth."

I thought about his hands in the shower, how good he'd been at helping me. "A slave?"

A rueful laugh flowed out of him. "Yes, that kind of slave, to a beautiful woman who had a cruel touch and a desire to shame me at every turn."

I bit my lower lip. "I would never do that to you."

He kissed me, his lips parting over mine, with so much care that my heart ached for him. He was afraid I would hurt him. That me, a tiny little human woman, would hurt this big, strong vampire man.

"Roll over," I whispered. "Let me show you what it is to be cared for."

Chapter Eleven

On the bed in my room, King rolled off me and onto his back, his hands going to his sides. I leaned over him. "Are you good with me taking the reins?"

He laughed. "Yes, though it hasn't been that way in a very long time."

I wanted to clap my hands with glee, but was afraid to startle him. It felt like I was dealing with a large uncertain beast that would bolt and run with any sudden movements.

I sat at his side and slid my hand down to the top of his damp pants. "May I remove these?"

He nodded, and I tugged the pants down, doing my best not to stare at the size and girth of him. Again, the urge to clap my hands and giggle almost overcame me, but I held it together. I was at his feet now, and I slowly climbed my way up his body, dragging my breasts and hair over his thighs, then over his straining cock, then up his chest until my pussy rested at the tip of him.

I took his hands and placed them on my breasts. "That's your only job."

"Terrible." He whispered, "What an awful task you give me."

I winked at him, and slid my hips back, pressing myself onto his cock, pressing him in the first few inches, and pausing. Good God, he was *huge*. Maybe I should have let Wick stretch me a little more.

His fingers flicked over my nipples, catching them and tugging them in a steady rhythm that my hips desperately wanted to match. I pushed down farther on him, my pussy tightening, pulling him in deeper.

"Sweet mercy." He groaned the words. "I won't—"

"Last, I know. You boys are all the same." I grinned down at him but the smile slid as I fought to take him all the way in. Maybe he wasn't longer than Preacher, but wider, and that stretching sensation of holding all of him brought me to the razor's edge of pleasure and pain as he filled me.

On my knees, I pulled away and pushed back in a long, deep thrusting stroke that drew a gasp from both of us at the same time. His fingers tightened over my breasts, and I had to stop for a breath.

"I'm not going to last," I whispered to him.

His eyes closed. "Damn it."

I bit my lower lip, trying to hold the sensations in one place and not let them overcome me. "I...I have to move, King. I want you so badly. Please."

"Yes, ride me, lovely lady. Take us to heaven."

I shifted my weight, beginning the ride that would carry both of us to the heights of pleasure. Angling my body a little, I could get the occasional rub of his pelvic bone across my clit, spiking the urge to move faster and harder. He tugged and pulled on my nipples in the same pounding rhythm, until there was no distinguishing between the pleasure in the various parts of my body. It was all around me and it was all I could do to hang on, keep moving, keep drawing him in deeper and deeper.

He cried out first, his body bucking against mine as if he'd throw me off, wild and spasming as his orgasm caught him.

I kept moving, kept riding that knife edge of pleasure, wanting it to last forever, but my body was not interested in letting me take it further. My pussy began to pulse, a shimmering orgasm seeming to cascade upward from the center of my body, through my belly and breasts, erupting as a scream from my lips.

I collapsed on his chest, sweat dripping down my sides. He rolled us over on the bed, one arm under my neck, the other in the crook of my waist. His cock was still in me, as my body milked him with the last tremors of my orgasm.

"Allianna, are you okay?" He kissed the sides of my face. I blinked up at him.

"Okay? That was amazing. King, you make me feel things I didn't think were possible."

He kissed me, deeply and sweet and still, oh, so carefully. "Thank you, that is...the best thing you could have given me besides your trust."

"Happy to oblige, sir." I grinned up at him. "Just wait till next time."

He laughed, a grin spreading over his face, flashing his fangs. I reached up and touched one with my thumb, drawing a shudder through him.

"Not that I mind," I said, "I wish...I wish that all of you could bite me. I get the feeling the sensation would be phenomenal."

His arms tightened around me. "Only the one you choose will have the pleasure of your blood during sex."

"I know. Spartan told me. It's like a bonding thing?"

He kissed my nose. "Yes, something like that."

A sigh slid from him. "I wish I could stay longer. But Celt will only leave you an hour or so to yourself before he will want his time with you."

I held him tightly when he moved to pull away. "Stay with me, talk to me a little while. I will only need a few minutes to myself to clean up."

His green eyes were still full of uncertainty but he obliged, spinning out his story, at least as much as he could in that short time.

Being a slave was something he'd known as long as he'd been alive. There had never been a time when he had been free, not until he'd been taken to Lily to be turned into a vampire. His looks, and quiet, well-trained demeanor had been what had drawn Lily to him, apparently. Of course, there was fire under the calm, but he didn't let it out often. He and Preacher were the two brothers who kept the other three in check.

Kept them from wreaking havoc.

"You do a good job," I said, curling my head against his chest. "Spartan defended you immediately. There was no question in him about your loyalty."

King rubbed a hand down my back, drawing little patterns with his fingers. "He is a bit of a conundrum, that one. When we found him, he'd been beaten by the other hive."

"Wait, there's more than one hive?" I lifted my head and King smiled.

"There are many hives, and many queens and even some kings. Over fifty, at last count. Ours is one of the largest which is why we got away with stealing him out from under their noses. He didn't belong with them. While he is a warrior, his heart is too strong and true to be a violent man. It would have killed him eventually, if he'd had to stay there."

I had to agree with King. From what I'd seen of Spartan, he was far from the maniac he'd looked like on my first impression of him.

We lay there, talking for a few more minutes before the door burst open and Celt sauntered in. "Still going at it, are we?"

I looked up at him from over King's body. "Just talking. You want to come and join?" King stiffened and I laughed, patting his cheek. "Not like that. I meant just talking."

Celt, though, stripped off his coat and boots and flung them to the side. "Don't tell me you got our King to open up? What magic do you wield, lass?" With a hop, he was on the bed, his head tucked between mine and King's.

"Are you and Wick related?" I asked the blond-haired, blue-eyed man.

He roared. "Why, because we be twins of one another?"

"Nah," I shook my head. "You both be cheeky bastards."

King laughed and sat up. "I'll leave you to her, Celt. And you aren't going to last, brother."

Celt made a swiping motion with his hand. "Please, I can outlast any of you. Always have, always will."

King snorted, and grabbed his pants from the floor. I watched as he drew them over his hips, covering himself. A sigh of regret slid through me. His eyes darted to mine and there was a world of words unsaid that passed between us before he spoke to Celt. Gratitude, and an understanding of where we stood with one another that was clear as crystal.

"You want to make it interesting?" King asked.

"A bet? Damn, you're on, lad!" Celt still stood on the bed and held out his hand to King. "I can last no matter what the lassie throws at me."

I stood, stretched and headed to the bathroom, shaking my head at them both. "You two work out the details. I'll be right back."

I closed the bathroom door behind me, and leaned against it, drawing a deep shuddering breath. When I was in the arms of one of the brothers, the danger to my life faded to nothing more than a distant memory. After Celt, I would have something of a break then, an hour before Spartan would come to take me for training. I had to make a plan, I had to start finding a way out. From what I could see, it was the only surefire way to make sure we all survived Terra.

There seemed to be no rush to the men's sharing of me, even though each of them was happy to have their turn. They also wanted to give me a little time to myself, and I could put that to use.

I rubbed a hand over my face and walked to the mirror. My eyes were bright, my skin had a lovely glow from all the sex, and here and there the love bites from King, Preacher, and Wick. They showed bright against my pale skin. I ran my hands over my body, checking for any soreness. Nothing. That magic drink was magic indeed. I wasn't hungry. I wasn't tired. I wasn't bruised as I knew I should have been.

I stepped into the shower, soaping down and washing away the smell of King from my skin. Not that I was bothered by it, but it seemed only reasonable when I was about to climb into the arms of another man.

If Cassie could only see me now, she'd be rooting me on. Telling me to take them all, and society be damned.

I flicked the water off and a towel was handed to me. I turned to see Celt standing there, most of his clothes still on. I gave him a mocking pout, and did my best to affect an Irish accent.

"Think that if ye keep yer clothes on that will keep ye safe from my lusty ways?"

He barked a laugh. "That be terrible, lass. And I'll take my clothes off when I'm good and ready and not a second before."

I lifted one shoulder and let it drop along with the edge of the towel, exposing one breast. His blue eyes slid from my face, to my rose-pink nipple that perked up even as he looked. I bit my lower lip. "Seeing as you aren't interested, perhaps I'll just take care of my own needs then. That okay with you?"

His eyes flew to my face. "What?" The word somewhat strangled and I casually made my way past him, trailing a hand over his face, then down his chest.

"You said you could hold out, and that sounds like a challenge to me. Perhaps I have a few tricks up my sleeve?" I dropped the towel. "Oops, no sleeves."

I raised my eyes to his, and gave him a slow, deliberate blink of my lashes.

"Ah, lass, I've held out against worse."

The words were strong, but the way he shifted his stance told me everything. I looked around the room, spying an overstuffed chair with a seat that could probably fit several people. While I didn't want to hurry Celt, I also knew the sooner we were done, the sooner I'd have my hour to myself. I felt bad about rushing this. I wanted it to last with him too. I wanted to enjoy him thoroughly. If I ever got the chance, I'd make it up to him.

I tried not to think about the trouble I'd get in if I was caught trying to escape.

A zing of adrenaline shot through me.

I reached the chair and bent at the waist, running my hands over the velvet material. "This will do just fine, I think."

I shimmied onto the chair and leaned back, my knees together. Celt stared at me from across the room, his chest hitching with breath. I pursed my lips together again, and ran my hands over my body, starting at my knees, moving up over my thighs, across my belly, and up to my breasts. I cupped them both, holding their weight a moment before I ran my thumbs over both nipples. I bit my lower lip and let out a moan. My body was so sensitized, I was almost certain I could come just by playing with my nipples at this point.

"Devil woman, you work for King, do you?" His words were full of heat, but also laughter. Like Wick, Celt was full of trickery and fun. Well, that made three of us.

I sighed and continued to let my hands rub across my breasts. "No. But you said you could hold out on me. I don't want you to hold out, Celt. I want you to fuck me until our bones turn to liquid from coming so hard."

His jaw dropped and I leaned back in the chair a little more. "But since you want to hold out, I'll get started without you."

Inch by inch, I let my legs drop to the sides, opening myself to him. Letting him see me as I slid my one hand between my legs and dipped two fingers into my pussy. I shivered and shimmied my hips a little for a better angle as I swept my fingers up and over my clit, doing a slow circle while I stared at him.

He closed the distance between us, clothing dropping with each step.

I arched an eyebrow when he reached to touch me. I lifted a foot and put the sole of it against the front of his shoulder. "No, I think you can watch for now."

His eyes bugged out further. "Lass, *that* is not fair."

"You already used your voice on me, brought me to orgasm without a touch."

He frowned. "Is that what you want?"

I dipped my fingers again. "No, I want you to want me, to not be able to hold back."

Celt dropped to his knees. "I do want you, lass, more than you know."

"Then watch, and I'll tell you when you can join in." I didn't tip my head back, but let my gaze rest on him as I swirled my fingers between my pussy and my clit. While it felt good, it was nothing to the pleasure of having a man cupping me, holding my nipples between his teeth while he fucked me hard. I sucked in a sharp breath, the image making my hips dance and buck.

He groaned, his hands on the side of the chair, gripping it until it groaned along with him.

"You be killing me, lass."

His words sobered me as nothing else could have. "No, that's the last thing I want." I sat up and he took my fingers that had been inside of me and sucked on them.

"Lass, you be the sweetest thing I have tasted in a very long time." He kissed my palm and I scooted forward so his head was at my shoulder level.

Our lips met, hard, angling and more than a little demanding. Because I wanted him to want me, to not be able to hold back like I'd said.

He pulled back a little from me. "Why is wanting you so important?"

I was surprised he'd want to talk in the middle of sex, I'd had to almost force the others. "Because...my ex used it against me. He acted like he was never interested, when I know he went to stripper bars. I know he..." I paused, feeling the pain of being rejected again as if it had just happened, "I know he preferred his hand and his porno movies over me."

Celt's eyes closed and a pained look slid over his face. "Lass, you were with the wrong man is all."

"Am I with the right one now?" I whispered back. "Are you going to cast me aside, Celt?"

He kissed me hard, demanding once more, biting at my lower lip and tugging it toward him before he spoke.

"Let me show you just how much I want you, lass."

Chapter Twelve

Celt's mouth came back to mine in a swell of heat and desire that curled around us, like adrenaline turned into pure, liquid lust. We were both suddenly frantic, clinging to one another as we tumbled off the chair to the cool hardwood below us. I didn't care that the floor was hard and cold, only that this man was with me and he wanted me as much as I wanted him.

His mouth slid from my lips and latched onto one nipple, sucking hard, rolling the tip of it between his teeth until I cried out, the pleasure pain exquisite in its intensity. I bucked my hips up and he drove into me, hard and fast, while still holding my nipple in his mouth.

I dug my nails into his back, wanting all his hardness in me, wanting to feel the slap of my back against the floor as he took me without being careful or cautious. King's lovemaking had been gentle, and sweet, but this was the intense power of lust unleashed. A good and royal fucking.

I dragged Celt's mouth back to mine, and buried my tongue deep, tangling it with his own. I wrapped my legs around his waist holding him tightly, never wanting to let him go.

There was no finesse to this, just raw desire, and it was beautiful in its own uncontained way. I sucked on one of Celt's fangs and his whole body shuddered. "Sweet merciful heavens." He groaned the words as I reached around and grabbed hold of his ass, urging him into me harder.

"Celt, don't stop, please don't stop. You feel so good inside me."

That was it, those words seemed to unsnap whatever control he had. He put his palms on either side of my head and used the leverage of the floor to slam in and out of me fast and hard, until our bodies were both slick with heat and sweat. I stared up at him, marveling at the strength in him, but also how even with losing control he still wasn't hurting me.

He was still making sure I was okay.

I lifted my hips and tightened my inner muscles with each powerful thrust of his body, fast and faster. I could feel him coming, on the edge of it, trying to hold back.

I pulled his head down to mine and bit the edge of his ear. "Come for me, Celt."

With a holler, he lost the last edge of control, and gave a final thrust before he collapsed onto me. His whole body trembled and shook, and I held him to me, stroking a hand through his hair.

"Celt?"

"Hmm." There was no movement from him, though his chest rose and fell.

"Just making sure I didn't kill you," I said.

His chest shook with laughter. "Damn it. I hate it when King is right."

He pushed himself up over top of me, kissed me and then shook his head. "I will have to redeem myself."

"What do you mean?" I sat up and gave him a solid frown. "What was wrong with that?"

"I came, and you didn't. I will never hear the end of it from the others now."

I wrapped my arms around his shoulders. "I won't tell them. Besides, that was far from a poor performance. I like it rough and hard sometimes. All this being careful is nice but," I shrugged, "as I keep trying to remind the others, I'm no virgin. I know what I want and like. A slap on the ass and a bite on the back of the neck has its place too."

His blue eyes were unaccountably serious. "No, you are no virgin."

"That a bad thing?" I quirked an eyebrow at him.

He smiled. "No, I just...damn it. I don't want you to get hurt, Allianna."

I put my mouth against his shoulder. "I don't either. Spartan will help me; maybe I can beat her."

"She's been fighting her whole life," Celt said. He rubbed his head against my shoulder. "God, I do not like this at all."

We lay there, clinging to each other, fear wrapping around us. I wanted to stay there and believe everything would be okay. But I knew the truth. It was not going to be okay, not if I didn't find a way to get out of here. There was no way I could beat the queen, which meant I had to put distance between me and these men who were working their individual ways into my heart.

Not love, I reminded myself, but still, I cared for them. That, I thought, was almost as dangerous as if I did love them.

"Spartan will be here soon," I whispered against his skin. "I need to find some clothes for fighting."

"Ah, lassie," he kissed me again, "heart of a lion in you, me thinks. I'll find you some clothes, you clean up."

I stood and he swatted my ass cheek, the sound and tingling from his hand stopping me in place. I had to clamp my legs together to keep from dropping right there and taking him skin on skin again.

"Does me heart good to see you like it a bit rough. Nothing wrong with a slap and tickle now and then." He bit my ass then and jumped forward. I spun and glared at him.

"Next time, you're going to be the one getting a spank." I pointed a finger at him. He grinned back at me.

"I'll count on it, lass."

Once more, I stepped into the bathroom. I washed up in record speed, knowing I would get clean again after my training with Spartan.

I toweled off and opened the door to the bedroom. Celt was dressed and he held up a skin-tight black tank top and what looked like black leggings.

"Very cat burglary," I said, taking the leggings from him first. "Think you can find me a bra?"

"What, and contain those beautiful, wild creatures?" He cupped a hand around my breast and gave it a gentle squeeze.

I fought the tightening of lust between my legs. I stepped back, my eyes on him. "You keep doing that and neither of us will be going anywhere."

His eyes narrowed. "Maybe that be a better plan than working with Spartan?"

I closed my eyes, doing my best to block him out. "I am going to do all I can to keep us alive, so I can fuck you whenever I want for the rest of my life." I opened my eyes, and Celt was right in front of me.

There may have been a glimmer of tears in his baby blues. "Yes, heart of a lion. If anyone can take the bitch queen down, I believe it will be you."

His faith in me, his words lifted me as nothing else could have. Not a kiss, not a touch, but a true and honestly spoken belief.

"Thank you." I leaned up and kissed him. "Now help me find a bra."

We pulled apart, and moments later he tossed me a black lacey bra. Once more, all the clothing fit me perfectly.

"How is it possible that this fits me?" I slid the top on. "You boys been watching me?"

Celt shook his head. "These are Lily's clothes. The only possible mate we could ever have would be made after her form."

I wasn't sure how I felt about that. Good, bad. Or just plain unsettled.

He stood at the door. "Wait for Spartan. He'll be here for you, lass. Don't leave the room without him."

I lifted a hand to wave, and just like that he was gone, and I was alone. I counted to sixty, though my heart was beating so fast I was sure it had been less than a minute.

The miniscule plan I had was not a very good one, but it was pretty much all I could come up with considering most of the blood in my body was circulating away from my brain the last couple of days.

In the room with the caged wolf there had been multiple weapons scattered around the floor. Not that I thought I would truly be able to fight my way out of here, but the reality was without a weapon, I was dead in the water. With a weapon, I at least had a chance. Spartan had said vampires could be killed just like any human. I only needed one clean shot.

Right, like I was one of my rip-snorting heroines come to life? Maybe I was delusional. Still, my plan didn't change, despite whatever doubts I had.

I went to the door of the room and opened it, peering out down the hallway to either side. No one was coming yet. I had maybe half an hour at best.

I hurried to the left, running as quickly as I dared in my soft-soled boots that Celt had laced up to my knees for me.

Down the stairs I went, almost tripping over my feet I was moving so fast. At the bottom of the stairs, I twisted to the left and followed the narrow halls until once more I stood outside the wolf's cage. I pushed the door open.

"It's me." Oh, what an idiot I was. Like the wolf would know who 'it's me' was. I drew a breath, instantly regretted it as the smell of the room hit my tongue, and pushed the door open wide.

The rattle of chains drew my eyes to the back of the room. "I'm going to try and escape, and I think that it would be best if you tried to go at the same time. Because if there is total chaos we will both have a chance." I rattled off the words, unable to slow them for fear the wolf would have changed its mind about not killing me. Or that Spartan was already looking for me.

As it was, I kept myself in the doorway and what I hoped was out of reach of the wolf. Of Spartan, I had no plan of dealing with him if he found me.

The hulking figure of the wolf crept forward until I could see it in the dull light of the hall. The eyes were that dark brown that on any dog would have been sweet and doe-eyed. I swallowed hard. "I'm thinking if I took your chain off, you'd be able to get away when the time comes?"

A whine slipped from its throat and it lay on the floor, rolled to its back and totally exposed its—make that *his*—belly to me. Steeling my spine, I took a step forward, and then another and another. The chain was clinched around his throat like a pinch collar. Every time he pulled, the interior of the collar tightened, and the dull spikes put pressure on his throat, essentially strangling him. I rested a hand on his shoulder.

"Hang on. I'll get this off."

I worked my hands through his thick fur, trying to find the opening of the latch. A very small part of me reminded me that I was being foolish, maybe even dangerously stupid. The rest of me reminded me that I couldn't very well leave this wolf here, not when I might die before I could free him for real. No one deserved to die locked away in a dungeon of filth.

What if he deserves to be here, what if he killed someone?

The thought bounced around my brain as my fingers finally found the latch and I flicked it open. Too late now to go back, to change my mind.

The sharp spikes had dug into his flesh under the fur, embedding themselves. "I'm sorry, this may hurt." I peeled the collar off, wincing as I did with the way it suctioned off him. The wolf never moved from where he lay on his back, though I did see a tremor run through his body.

I tossed the collar to the side, and the clatter of the iron on the stone walls seemed to fill the small space. The wolf stayed there, though, just lying flat on his back.

"Wolf?"

He rolled to his side and as he rolled, his body...contorted, shifting until it was no wolf standing in front of me but a buck-naked man. I stumbled back a few steps out of shock more than anything else. Not like I hadn't seen my share of naked men lately, and his body was as fine as any of them.

His face was unlined, and I would have placed him around my age or even younger if not for the bright gray of his hair that was shorn close to his head. Those brown eyes swept over me as he frowned. "Who are you that you would defy Terra?"

I looked over my shoulder. "I don't have much time. My name is Ally, and...there's a good chance I might die in the next couple of days. But I'm going to try and make a break for it in four days."

He nodded. "How will I know?"

A flash of inspiration hit me. "Do you know this place at all, like can you find your way around the hive?"

His jaw tightened and flexed before he answered. "Unfortunately, yes."

"The hospital, if you can get there, my friend Cassie will be waiting. She'll be killed too if I die."

He took a step closer. "You are going to face the queen then? You are one of the women to try and unseat her?"

I nodded. "That's the plan, but I am no fighter, which means I'm pretty much walking to the gallows."

He squinted his eyes. "But you are a thinker. And she's dumb as a bag of rocks."

I bit my lower lip to keep from laughing. "Yeah, I don't like her much either."

He held out his hand. "My name is Havoc. I am Alpha of the Windrun pack."

I shook his hand. "Nice to meet you, Havoc. Try not to scare Cassie. She's a good person with a mean right hook."

He shrugged. "I will do my best not to frighten her and avoid her fists." I bent to pick up one of the weapons and he stopped me.

"No. They will recognize the weapons and know you were here with me. Go, I will slip up to the hospital when the small hours of the night come and the vampires feast."

I swallowed hard. Shit, that was a part of the brothers' lives I really had tried not to think on too much. They most certainly weren't feeding on me, but that meant they were feeding on someone.

Havoc gave my shoulder a gentle push. "Go, Ally, and I will pray that you survive so we may escape together." He ushered me out the door and shut it in my face. I turned and ran back the way I'd come. I may not have gotten a weapon, but I perhaps I'd found something even more valuable.

An ally for Ally.

Chapter Thirteen

I hit my bedroom door, breathless from the flat-out sprint. I hadn't bothered to try and be stealthy on my way back. For all anyone knew, I was hurrying back to my room to get my time with one of the five men. I didn't stop running until I was through the door, and leaning against it.

My eyes closed, I worked to slow my breathing.

"Allianna."

A strangled squawk was all I managed as my eyes flew open to find Preacher there, sitting on the edge of the bed, watching me.

I bit my lower lip. "Hey."

"You went outside the room again? Why?"

God, here it was. I either lied and he would know it because I was a damn shitty liar or I told the truth.

I hung my head but kept my distance. "I...I am trying to find a way to make sure we all survive, Preacher." My voice caught on the words, the emotion as real and as raw as anything I'd ever felt. "I don't want to tell you more than that. Can you trust me to keep this to myself, to try and save us all?"

He took a few steps and then his hands were cupping my face, tilting my head so I was looking into those deep blue eyes. All I could do was think of him, and how quickly I had come to care for him and the boys. Those were my thoughts and I clung to them desperately to keep him from seeing anything else inside my head.

"I trust you, but I fear for you too. The other vampires do not want to lose their queen, Allianna. She has gone to war with the wolves, and allowed our kind to attack them at will. Their blood is...it is a powerful drug to us, addictive in nature." He made a face like he was embarrassed by the fact.

That sort of explained Havoc in the basement, though. Not only was he someone important but he tasted good, too. My writer brain went down that side path immediately. Someone important, held against his will for ransom while Queen Cunt did whatever she pleased to his pack. "Was it always like that? Fighting between them?"

Preacher shook his head. "No, they were our allies many years ago, before we lost Lily." He motioned for me to open the door. "I'm to take you to Spartan for your training. He'll bring you back here—"

"Can I go to your room after my training?"

He startled. "It's very small and mostly full of books. I'm not sure—"

"I'd like to see it, to see a piece of your life." Because I knew if I managed to escape, if I managed to get away, it would save them all, but I would never see any of them again. My throat tightened and I could barely swallow past the sudden lump. The thought that I would not laugh with them, would not hold them again, would not make love to them again. The pain pierced me, making it more than a little difficult to keep up with Preacher's long legs.

Preacher either didn't notice my distress, or chose not to comment. Ten minutes later, we were at the training ground.

Preacher turned and left me without a word. I couldn't deny the hurt that caused, and for a moment, I thought he would come back, and tell me he'd noticed me being upset or that he didn't mean to hurt me.

Less than a minute after he left, I realized what had happened.

I slapped a hand against my forehead. "You are a moron, Ally."

Preacher could read my mind, and I'd been thinking about escaping, about getting away. He might even realize what I'd told Havoc, that I was trying to help him escape too.

Now Preacher knew. No wonder he'd been pissed with me.

My shoulders slumped as Spartan strode across the field to me. "Ally, you are late."

"Not really a time limit on this, is there?" I snapped at him, my upset and irritation flooding me.

"Actually, there is, seeing as we are down to three and a half days before you face the queen." He held out his hand to me, offering me a small knife.

I didn't take it. "I thought you said hand to hand."

"Yes, but this will make you more cautious, I think." He frowned at me. "Have you been crying?"

I rubbed my hands over my face. "On the way here, I was thinking about escaping, and what it would mean, that I would never see any of you again, but at least you would all be alive."

His eyebrows shot up. "That's a bit more honest than I would have thought from you."

A sigh slid from me. "Preacher brought me here. I'm sure he will tell all of you, and no doubt I'll have a guard on my door from now on."

"Escape is not possible," Spartan said. "You'll have no guard because you won't be able to get away. Sorry to burst your little bubble."

I frowned at him. "I'm smarter than I look."

His lips twitched. "I'm sure you are."

"I am an author, I'll have you know. I'm quite sure I could come up with an escape plan better than anything you could come up with." I poked a finger into his chest. "For all you know, I've already begun digging a tunnel out from my room. A tunnel I hide under one of those cheap-ass posters with a half-naked man on it."

That earned me a full-bellied laugh from him.

Which only made me frown harder. "It's not that funny."

"Oh, Ally, it is. I was a strategist. I know how to set up troops, how to make an assassination look like a natural death. I know how to get out of the worst situations."

Anger snapped through me at the condescending tone that all but dripped from his mouth. I'd show him.

"Yet, here you are, stuck with me in this situation where if *I* don't do something, at least four of your brothers and myself will be dead before the week is out. Well done. Should I clap for you?"

Our eyes locked and it was not a sexy, come-hither look that either of us had. Anger and tension snapped between us. His hands clenched tightly and then he flicked the knife away, burying the blade into the soft turf of the field.

"Our session is done. Good luck with the queen." Spartan brushed past me, shouldering me bodily out of the way.

Tears sprang to my eyes. "Thanks for nothing, asshole." I stood, watching him go, my heart and mind racing.

He'd shown me the forms of how to defend myself. Just because he wasn't with me didn't mean I couldn't practice. Because if I couldn't get away, I was going to be in the fight for my life far sooner than I wanted.

I turned my back on him and settled into a balanced stance. I lifted my hands and began to work through the flowing forms of blocking and striking, over and over, until the sweat rolled down my face, the salt of it stinging my eyes. I didn't stop, I didn't slow. Unlike Spartan, I would do something with my last few days. I would fight to save us all.

Dumb-ass man and his dumb-ass pride.

I was so intent on the motions of the flow, of prepping myself for battle against a queen who would likely wipe the floor with me, that I didn't see the figures creeping closer from the edges of the field.

A slow clap stopped me in mid-block with an imaginary opponent. I looked to my right to see Malcom approaching. His blue eyes were full of...irritation? Humor? I wasn't sure if he was happy I was there, or if he wanted to just kill me where I stood. Maybe both.

I stood up straight and put my hands on my hips. "You want another round of having your balls smashed up into the back of your mouth? 'Cause that's the mood I'm in today. I will have zero of your shit. I will take none of your garbage, and for all I care you can fuck off and die."

He probably didn't deserve all of that. It was Spartan I was pissed with, not Malcom. Though I could blame Malcom for bringing me here in the first place and putting me in this mess.

He smiled, but there was no warmth in it, and his words echoed my own thoughts. "No thank you for bringing you here? That's rude, Allianna."

I shrugged. "You never asked. You took without even questioning what I wanted."

"That's not how it works in our world. Which is why right now, I'm going to have a taste of your sweet, hot blood."

He leapt at me, half-flying through the air, his arms out wide. I dropped to my knees, and rolled to where Spartan had tossed the knife. I didn't think Malcom meant to take a sip of my blood but the whole damn lot of it. I caught the handle of the knife in mid-roll, and came up swinging, praying something of Spartan's teaching had stuck with me.

I arced the blade out, wildly, and managed to catch Malcom across the chest as he lunged at me, his fangs bared.

Snarling, he fell back and put a hand to the wound. "You wicked bitch."

"Takes one to know one." I stayed in a crouch with the knife held out in front of me. The only thing I could think was at least I wasn't shaking. Malcom might kill me, but I would not go down cowering.

He circled me, his hands wide. "You think you can take me?"

"Again? Probably." I fired the words, and the other vampires around us laughed at his expense. His face tightened into a snarl that twisted his handsome features into an image of hatred so strong that if I hadn't been fighting for my life I would have been afraid.

As it was, I circled with him, watching his body the way Spartan had taught me. A part of my brain pointed out that in its own way, this was excellent practice for facing Terra. Assuming Malcom didn't kill me outright.

Malcom shot out a hand, and I tried to block it, and ended up on my back, with Malcom on top of me. So much for holding him off.

I drove my elbow into the crook of his neck, and tried to throw him from me.

"Ah, she likes it rough," he growled, reared up and then struck, biting deeply into my shoulder. I couldn't stop the scream. The pain was so sharp, as though he'd not just cut through skin but somehow sliced into my bone, breaking me open. He shook his head like a dog, or a shark, as if he would try and pull a hunk of my shoulder off.

I didn't stop fighting, though. I couldn't. This was my life on the line.

With my other hand, I reached for his face, going for his eyes. I caught the edge of one and drove my fingers as hard I could into it. He howled and pulled off me, and I managed to skitter backward.

Where was Spartan, or King, or Preacher? Where were Wick and Celt? The men who had said they would protect me were absent at the worst possible time.

Here I was again, on my own. Another time, I would analyze the fact that I seemed drawn to men who left me out to dry.

Blood slid down my top, warm and wet from the wound in my shoulder. My free hand clutched at the grass; miraculously, I found the handle of the knife.

I stood again and settled into a fighting stance once more. There was a chorus of oohs from the other vampires.

One of Malcom's eyes was shut tightly but the other glared at me. "You—"

"Bitch, I know. I heard you the first time," I snapped. Fear cut through me. I was not ready to die. I did not want to go out like this.

"No." Malcom gave me a nod. "You're stronger than I gave you credit for."

I didn't want praise from him. "Fuck off, Malcom."

"Can't." There was something sad in his voice. "Fuck, I can't. Orders are orders."

Malcom's legs tensed and I readied myself. I wouldn't be so lucky this time as to keep him off me.

He was in the air; the world around us seemed to freeze. I knew this was the moment he'd take me down, bury his fangs in my neck and drain me.

I was about to die.

A blur from the side and a new body entered the fray, tackling Malcom just before he slammed into me. I didn't dare back up. Malcom's friends were there, waiting on the edge of the circle. Which meant I had a front-row seat to the battle in front of me.

I blinked, trying to see what was happening, but the bodies moved so fast, I could see nothing but bits and pieces, arms, legs, a shake of dirty blond hair.

"Spartan." I breathed his name. He came back for me. Or had he heard me cry out? I clutched the knife, all but dancing on my toes because I didn't know what to do. There was no way for me to help without potentially causing more grief.

There was a sudden scream of pain and the two men parted, one standing, the other curled on the ground around his middle.

Spartan didn't look over his shoulder at me, but instead put a booted foot on Malcom's neck, pressing him into the ground. "Apologize to her."

Malcom groaned. "I am the queen's man and I have my orders. You know that well."

"Which are what?" I closed the distance between us. "What are her orders concerning me?"

Malcom's eyes flicked to me and away. "That if any of us were to catch you on your own, we were to kill you on sight. Or at the very least drain you of enough blood to weaken you for the fight."

He shuddered. "I do not want her as a queen, but she is a Pusher. You know that, Spartan, you and your brothers are the only ones who can stand against her demands."

Pusher, what did that mean exactly? I quickly put his words together, understanding dawning despite the throbbing ache in my shoulder. "She can control you?"

"Yes." Spartan lifted his foot from Malcom's neck and came around to me. When he moved to take my arm, I jerked away from him, wincing.

"No. You don't just get to come in here, save me, and think that everything from before is better."

I steeled my shoulders, thoughts racing. "I'm going to see Cassie."

I walked away from him, limping, my body announcing new injuries with every step. I didn't care. I was leaving right then, before there was another attempt on my life.

Before Spartan broke my heart again with his callous words.

Chapter Fourteen

Spartan did not follow me from the training field, nor did any of the other vampires. I reached the narrow passageways and broke into a run, finding the hospital with only one wrong turn that I had to backtrack. I burst through the door, out of breath, and my adrenaline flowing hot, which I think was one of the few things keeping me standing. The injury to my shoulder throbbed with a beat all its own, and from what I knew that was not a good thing.

"Cassie?" I called out, not caring how loud I was. I knew an opening when I saw one, and this moment was it. This was our chance to get away.

My friend sat up and stared at me with ever-widening eyes as she took me in, the wound and the blood. "Ally, what happened?"

"Where is the doctor?"

She shook her head. "Gone, called away."

"And the other patients?" I asked even as I searched the room. Far as I could see, the other patients were gone, the chains hanging empty. Eaten? Probably.

The bite wound in my shoulder ached and throbbed with a pain I suspected was only going to get worse.

Already I could feel the heat from the bite curling down my arm and upper back—an infection was brewing at an inhuman speed.

"Is Havoc here?" I asked. I'd not given him a lot of time. I could only hope that it was enough.

I turned as he stepped out from behind a tall storage cabinet and gave me a tight smile. "I am."

I nodded. "Now or never, then. Help me block the door. We need to buy ourselves more time."

His lanky form was covered with pale green scrubs, but I could see his own injuries bleeding through here and there.

He glanced at the bite on my shoulder. "If we can get you to my pack, we can heal that infection."

"Thank you," I said as I helped him move a an exam table in front of the door.

"The least I can do. I was set to be killed as a sacrifice to the new queen."

I snorted and waved at my shoulder. "No new queen happening here."

Cassie stood on the bed under the long skylight. "If Havoc can lift me up, I can get into the chimney."

He went to the bed and climbed up next to her. "You have the hammer?"

She touched a small reflex-testing hammer in her belt. "Got it. Ready to break out."

With ease he scooped her up, his hands on her ass as he benched her over his head. She scrambled up and he continued to help her, his hands under her legs, feet and then she was free of him and in the chimney.

Havoc glance at me. "You next."

The door behind us rattled. I hurried to him and he hoisted me into the air over his head. With effort, I got myself into the chimney, pressing my back on the one side and walking up with my feet on the other side. I tried not to hear the shouting below. Tried not to hear Spartan's voice, or Preacher's, King's, Wick's or Celt's. They were calling to me.

Trying to stop me from leaving.

I kept moving. "I'm saving you all," I whispered.

Havoc leapt up into the chimney with a single jump, digging his hands and bare feet into holds that I couldn't even see. He was right under me. "If you fall, I'll catch you."

"You'd better," Cassie snapped down. "She's my best friend. I'm not losing her now."

I looked up to see her swing the hammer at the same time as the door far below us shattered open. Glass tinkled down around us, and I could only hope we still had enough time.

God, let us have enough time that my leaving would save my boys. My heart jumped hard in my chest at the sudden truth. My boys, even Spartan was in that mix. I wanted them all, and I would do this to free them from danger.

Havoc pushed me from below and I got moving again.

Moments later Cassie helped me up and out of the tight chimney, and then Havoc was there and we were standing in the middle of a deep green forest. A full moon peeked here and there through the trees.

"Run," Havoc growled.

Cassie and I broke into a run. I'd always been faster than her, even when I was heavier. But now she had to slow to keep pace with me.

"It's the wound," Havoc said. "The wound is slowing her down."

I tried to swallow, to tell them I could keep up, but I could barely get the spit down my throat. I struggled to breathe.

From behind us came shouting, the sound of a snarl.

I fell to my knees and Havoc moved to pick me up. I shook my head. "Save her. Save her."

His brown eyes softened. "Fight for them, Ally. You're stronger than you know."

He spun and grabbed Cassie by the hand. She cried out for me, but he overpowered her and in a split second they were gone, eaten up by the dark of the forest.

"Be safe, be happy, my sweet friend." They were the last words I managed before I slumped forward, my face pressed into the cool night grass.

Frost tickled my nose and I wondered at it because I did not feel cold at all. If anything, I wanted to strip my clothes off and let my body cool from this intense burning heat.

Someone was calling to me. Was it my mother? I wasn't sure, but I remembered she was dead, both her and Dad in the car accident. Which meant that if I was hearing her, maybe I was dying too? Was it possible... maybe...I didn't know. Worse, I wasn't sure I cared.

If I died, my men would be safe. I didn't think I'd spoken them, but the response was as if I had. Then again, Preacher would have heard my thoughts if he were close enough, and he could relay them to the others. I floated in and out of the fog.

"Ah, Allianna." Someone choked on my name. King, it was King I'd upset.

I managed to open my eyes. The five men who'd so quickly worked their way into my heart and mind surrounded me. That wasn't true; Spartan stood back a few feet staring at the ground.

I drew a slow breath, but I couldn't speak. *Am I dying?*

Preacher nodded. "Yes, Allianna. You're dying. Malcom's bite is poison."

Havoc said his people could cure me. That they could save me.

Preacher startled and relayed my thoughts to the other four. They began to argue, and I could feel time slipping away, could feel my life counted in minutes left to me, not hours or days. It was Spartan who stepped forward and scooped me into his arms.

"I was wrong about her. I've been trying to prove she's like all the other women we've known. Those who wanted the throne, but didn't give a shit about us. I've denied her time and again and I've been wrong. I won't let her die now that I've pulled my head out of my ass."

There was a rush of movement and the world shot by me. He was running, still holding me. I had the feeling that the others were not far behind.

I wasn't sure how long the run was. One moment we were in full motion, the next we were still and there was the sound of deep rolling growls all around us.

"Havoc, Ally saved you," Spartan called out. "I would have you return the favor and save her life. If you still can."

The growling intensified and then I was snatched from Spartan. I let out a whimper and reached for him, but he was swept away from me under a tidal wave of fur and fangs.

Don't hurt him. Don't hurt him.

"Shush, save your energy," a grumbling voice muttered. "Open your mouth, princess."

I cracked my mouth open and a hot, vile liquid was jammed into it. I gagged, tried to turn my head but was held down until every last drop was swallowed, forced down my throat.

That vile taste was nothing, though, to the next thing that happened.

My shoulder was lanced. I turned my head in time to see a jet-black claw raked across my shoulder.

Pus burst out of the wound, green and smelling of death. I screamed, the pain rocketing through me not from the claw but resonating from deep within my shoulder.

"Poison bite, this was done on purpose," that grumbling voice said. "It'll ease, princess. It'll ease."

"Let me see her!" Cassie yelled, suddenly at my side, clutching at my good hand. "I'm here. I'm here."

I closed my eyes, fatigue washing over me. Whatever was in the magic drink Preacher had given me on my first day could not stand up to this injury, and the counteractive measures against it.

Sleep slipped over me and I did not fight its call. Cassie would stand up for me, and so would my men, and Havoc I was sure would, too, if it came down to it.

The dreams that found me in that dark abyss were strange and called me through the shadows of my mind.

I saw Havoc and six other shadows circling Cassie. I saw my sister Dominique standing with four men. I saw her best friend Rose die, killed by an explosion a year ago, and yet she was here, surrounded by spirits. All the images had a sense of danger around them...danger and love, too, as strange as that seemed. I reached for Cassie and Dominique, wanting to tell them, to warn them, not to go toward the supernatural I saw waiting for them, that their lives would be in danger, no matter how the bonds of love pulled at them.

Love. I wanted to snort at myself. I was not in love with the five vampires.

Why not?

The question from my own mind shocked me. Why not indeed? Was there such a thing as love at first sight? Or in this case, love at first fuck? But I hadn't bedded Spartan, and my emotions around him were as tangled and complex as the ones wrapped around the other four men. Maybe even a little more, if I were being honest. Because I did not truly know where I stood with him, and yet I understood him. I wondered at his ability to deny the heat between us.

A groan slipped from my mouth and several hands pressed against my body, holding me down.

"Let the curative work." Again, that growling deep voice. A part of my brain went to my writing. That voice belonged to an old man, bent at the back, magic flowing in his veins. A healer or a shaman.

I struggled up out of the pulse and flow of the curative. "I need to be awake."

"You need to heal." The hands pushed me down, gently, but with strength I could not deny. Five hands, to be exact. One on each limb, and the last between my breasts.

My five men.

I managed to flicker my eyelids and catch a glimpse of the scene above me. King and Wick stood holding my arms. Celt and Preacher were on my legs, and Spartan had his hand on my chest.

Spartan leaned over me. "Sleep, we will protect you."

"First time," I mumbled. I wanted to say first time for everything but that was all I managed. Spartan nodded.

"Yes, first time for everything. We are with you now, Ally. We are your guardians. We will not let this happen again. We were foolish to underestimate you."

I wanted to say that the queen might have something to say about that. I also wanted to point out we were wasting valuable time. I could be training. Or we could be planning some sort of plan. Succinct, even for me.

But what was that time going to do for us? Would I train to fight the queen and hope that I could win?

Would I allow myself to enjoy my fist of men until my life was ended in a few short days?

Or could I convince them to go with me, to run from the queen and live out our lives elsewhere?

"Sleep," Preacher said, "and we will discuss all of it when you wake."

His words acted as a release, and I cascaded into the depths of sleep as though falling from the top of a mountain, knowing there would be men I was tumbling head over heels in love with at the bottom to catch me.

Chapter Fifteen

I don't know how long I slept, only that as I woke, my body had an instant craving for being touched, to be held. I arched upward, sitting upright in a single smooth motion. The rough sheet covering me slid off my upper body and pooled at my waist. Naked from the waist up, the cool breeze made my skin prickle and my nipples harden.

Taking in the room, I noted the hanging dried herbs and flowers, the tinkling of seashells hanging on thin strings that could be sinew, the smell of incense and the crackling of a fire. I looked at my shoulder where Malcom had bitten me.

The wound was healed; the scars, though, were bright pink and still angry-looking, running outward like a sunburst. I ran a finger over them, marveling at the speed of how it had closed.

Unless...was it possible that I'd been asleep for weeks? Would the queen have forgotten about me, or maybe even just have let me go?

"Feeling better?" The grumbling voice turned me around.

An old man with white hair that stretched to his lap in tight dreadlocks stared at me. His dark eyes reminded me of a raven, or a crow, the solid black glittering and full of intelligence. He was covered in a light brown fur robe over his shoulders, a twisted staff in his one hand.

"You saved my life." I pulled the sheet up to cover my breasts.

"I did. And you don't have to bother covering up. I've seen it all." He waggled his eyebrows at me.

I laughed softly. "I'm sure you have. Still, give me the pretense of being modest."

"Ha, this from the woman who has finally tamed the final five."

I blinked a few times, his words settling in. "Tell me what you know of them, of the situation I'm in. They are bound by secrets and rules. I'm thinking you aren't."

He grinned at me, perfect white teeth flashing. "Yes, you would make a far better queen than Terra. I see it in your heart. And that wicked sharp mind of yours." He bobbed his head. "I'll tell you what I can, and I'm going to teach you how to block that Preacher boy from your mind while we're at it. You might need to keep him out at some point."

"That Preacher boy saved my life," I pointed out. "If he had not known my thoughts, I would not be alive."

The old man snorted. "But you might have gotten away fully if he hadn't realized you wished to save them by escaping."

He had a point that I conceded with a tip of my head in his direction. "Tell me what you can, old fart."

A barking laugh escaped him, and when I say barking, I mean, I looked around for the dog in the room, then finally back to him. It was one thing to acknowledge

Havoc for what he was in my mind. "You're a," shit, I could not believe I was going to say this out loud, "werewolf?"

"You seem shocked, you who has been living with vampires the last few days." He snorted, and shook his head at me which produced a tinkling noise. Beads woven into the long ends of his hair clanked together, producing the sound I'd previously thought was the sea shells on strings.

I shrugged. "I'm not and I am. I mean, I've lived in these worlds inside my head for so long, it seems strange to have them playing out in front of me in real time. They were always real to a degree, I suppose, but one does not expect to suddenly walk out their door and into a fairy tale."

He watched me closely. "You feel this is a fairy tale?"

A sigh slid from me. "I do not expect a happy ending."

He grinned. "Well, maybe I can help with that. Let me tell you of the vampires, and just what you've been caught up in, my young princess."

"I'm no princess."

His grin never slipped. "You are. And hopefully we can see you made into a queen."

With a shifting of his weight, he settled back into his chair and set his staff in front of him. With the tip, he drew in the loose soil of the earth at his feet.

I slid from the table, wrapped the sheet around my body and went to my knees in front of him to watch. The swirls in the soil condensed and grew into images, and scenes that matched the words he spoke.

"The previous queen, Lillianna, was as good a queen as the vampires had ever had. Out of all the hives, she was the fairest, and showed great kindness to all her men. She reached out to our pack, and we created a beneficial tie with them. We protected the borders, and when we had need of help with the humans, the vampires aided us. Then the hundred-year trial came upon us. A young, violent girl of just eighteen claimed her consort, and killed Lillianna."

I held up a hand, stopping him. "Is there always a fight for the throne every hundred years?"

"Yes. It isn't just law, but a way of keeping the bloodlines clean and strong. But Lillianna had been willing to step down if she thought the new queen would be good to her hive. Something which is acceptable. She would have taken her chosen consort and lived out her life as long as she wished in peace. She should not have been killed. It was not her time, and everyone here knew it."

He sighed. "As it was, Terra killed her instead. She wanted no one to gainsay her rule. Since then, she has been on a rampage, alienating her hive from our pack, and doing all she could to take over other hives. Now here we are at the cusp of a new queen," he looked at me. "Terra has killed the other four women who were brought before her. You are our last hope to stop her, and save not only the vampires, but our pack from her wrath as well."

I leaned back and drew a slow breath. "I am not strong enough. I couldn't even stand up to Malcom." I waved a hand at the sunburst scar on my shoulder.

"Bah, you do not know that. Besides, you are not alone. You have your fist." He held up his one hand and ticked off his fingers. "Five men with you at the center," he closed the fingers into a tight fist to emphasize his words. "You are stronger together than any of you realize."

A tiny burst of hope opened in my chest. "How long do I have before I must face her?"

"Twenty-four hours, give or take." He made a wobbling motion with his hand. "You are their hope, Ally. Will you try to win?"

I closed my eyes. "My sister Dominique. Someone needs to tell her what happened to me...if I fail."

"It will be done."

"And what about Cassie?"

He grinned wide. "Ah, well, her story is not over yet. I believe she has a role to play in our world too."

My eyes narrowed. "Don't you dare hurt her."

He continued to grin. "I would not hurt her for all the power in the world. She is like you, a woman unaware of her potential to change the world around her. I like her. She's spicy. And you were right, she has a mean right hook, according to Havoc."

Laughter tickled up my throat. "Yeah, that she does." I rubbed a hand over my face. "Do you have any other advice?"

"To block the Preacher from your mind, you must only say these words: From my mind, I cast thee."

I blinked. "Seems too easy."

He shrugged. "A great deal of magic is simpler than you might want to believe."

I stood, wobbled a little, and grabbed the edge of the bed. "Okay, so I have to kill Terra the Twat. That will solve all the problems?"

"She cheats in her fights. It is how she beat Lillianna."

I groaned. "Of course she does, the twats always cheat. Damn it." I rubbed my face again.

There was quiet except for the crackling of the fire for a solid minute before he spoke again.

"You could call on the spirit of Lillianna to help you win."

I turned and looked at him. "What?"

"Lillianna was a great fighter, and only lost to Terra because she cheated. If you allowed Lillianna's spirit to join with yours you might have a chance."

"Yeah, but what does that entail? Chicken blood and dancing naked beneath the moon?"

He gave another of his barking laughs. "Hardly." He stood and brushed past me to a work table on the far side of the room. "Here, take this, drink it right before the fight."

He held out a flask to me. The bottle was tiny, and would fit in the palm of my hand. I did not reach for it. "What is it?"

"Essence of Lillianna. If you are meant to be the new hive queen, you will be able to accept her spirit into your body. The fluid in this," he shook the flask, "will open that conduit. I've been saving it, hoping that I could help change the direction of the hive. She left it with me, when she saw that Terra would be taking her place."

I took the flask gingerly. "So there aren't really bits and pieces of her in here?"

"No." He chuckled. "Though perhaps it would be more believable if that was the case."

There was a soft shuffle at the door and then a firm rap of knuckles on the wood. The old man grunted. "Your men are not patient when it comes to you."

I thought about how each of them had struggled to last in bed with me. "That's an understatement."

The knock came again. The old werewolf shuffled to the door and swung it open. A blast of winter curled in, snow in the air, and a brilliant white haze behind the man in the doorway.

King stepped in, his arms full of material that I could only guess was a dress. A deep red dress with masses of crinoline skirts. It spilled over his arms and trailed on the floor.

"Allianna, are you well?" His green eyes were full of concern, and I wanted nothing more than to throw myself at him, to have his gentle touch soothe away the last of the aches in my body and the lingering fear in my heart.

I nodded, my eyes welling up. I hadn't even noticed the old werewolf slipping out but suddenly King and I were alone.

"I didn't...I was just trying to..." I struggled with the words because an apology wouldn't be sincere. I wasn't sorry I'd tried to save them, not for a single second.

He stepped close to me and put the dress on the bed so he could wrap his arms around me. "Don't. We know why you did it. You are the first to fight for us, to truly try and save all of us. For that...we will die for and with you if we must."

I frowned up at him. "What do you mean, the first?"

His jaw ticked. "I thought Ralph explained everything we could not?"

"Ralph?"

The door burst back open and the old werewolf grunted. "Yes, Ralph. It's a shit name but I didn't give it to myself. That one last bit, I forgot to tell you. There are no other fists remaining with competing girls for the queen's position. Only one. Which means four other girls bedded these big boys and tried to take the throne."

My heart tightened. "But there...the queen kills not only the woman who faces her, but her consort too."

King nodded. "There were nine brothers to start. Two fists."

I gasped, understanding flowing through me and making me ache for them. "That is why Spartan was so angry I was there. You've already lost four brothers?"

"Yes." King's hands smoothed down my back. "He thought another of us would die, and then we would be reduced to four, or worse, we would all be killed."

"That was not Lillianna's rule, was it?"

He shook his head. "Terra put that rule in place because she hates us. We were Lillianna's favored sons, and we have stood in Terra's way time and again, because we could resist her ability to control us. We have done what we could to stop her. This is her punishment for us, to force us to watch each other die."

I pressed my forehead against his chest, hurt and understanding in equal measure filling me. I was not special to them. They had done the same thing with each woman. I was nothing more than their last chance at survival. I let a slow breath out, and with it I pushed away the jealousy.

More was at stake than my feelings of hurt, than my feeling of inadequacy. Lives and futures were at stake, and I was not a child to let my own insecurities get the better of me.

"I should get dressed then. Though why this monstrosity?"

"You are going to be seen by the wolves, and you must do so in the expected garb of a princess of the hive."

My jaw ticked. First time I'd been called princess was by King, but now it felt...like an arrow instead of an endearment.

King didn't seem to pick up on my shift in emotions, or if he did, he said nothing. His hands were sure and quick as he helped me step into the voluminously long dress. The corset of the dress peaked above each breast, and dipped low between them like exaggerated mountains. The material of the corset was glittering red scales that overlapped and hugged my curves tightly. From just below my waist, the skirts fanned outward into a huge sweep. Shorter at the front so I wouldn't trip over my own feet, the skirt made up for it at the back with what had to be close to fifteen feet of train.

I touched the dress. "Can we not just leave? We are free of the hive, why can't we just go?"

"The queen knows we are here. If we do not return, she will send her guards after us and slaughter us all where we stand."

So much for that idea. I tried another direction, anger snapping through me.

"A bit ridiculous for walking back to the hive, isn't it?" I arched an eyebrow at King. Did he love the other girls? Did he miss them? Was he hurt when they died or was he happy?

He frowned and brushed a hand over my forehead. "I wish I could read your mind like Preacher. I see questions and worries in your eyes like storm clouds hovering."

He bent forward and tried to kiss me. I turned my head, so he grazed my cheek instead of my lips.

"Allianna?" He whispered my name and it tugged at me like nothing else could. I shook my head, my hair cascading over my bare shoulders and upper back.

"I can't, King. Not right now."

"Of course." He gave me a half-bow and I wasn't sure if he was mocking me, and that hurt me all over again. Damn this entire situation.

He helped me with thigh-high boots that encased my legs in the softest of red leathers. The interior was lined in thick white fur that would keep me warm.

I swallowed all my trepidation and spoke before I lost my nerve. "I want to speak to the wolves before we leave."

"I don't think that's a good idea." He shook his head. "They don't like us all that much right now."

I stiffened my spine. "None of this has been a good idea, but it is where we are and I am doing all I can to make this right."

He bowed his head and it took all I had not to run my fingers through it, and tug him toward me.

"As you wish." He held the door open and I walked into the brilliant white snow to get my first glimpse of the new world that waited for me.

Chapter Sixteen

The bright white of new snow dusting the ground and trees around us dazzled my eyes after the darkness of Ralph's healing room.

Ralph the werewolf healer. The words were too funny in my stressed-out state and I had to stifle a nervous giggle.

The urge to laugh faded as I took in the scene around me. We were at one end of a clearing ringed with huge trees, and within that circle stood people—or maybe a more accurate term would be werewolves. More than one of them had the look of Havoc when he'd been chained in the hive. Their hulking bodies, thick fur, and open jaws making their stance clear. They were not all happy that we were here.

Celt, Wick, Spartan and Preacher waited for me off to the left. They shared a look with King who shook his head. I held my head high.

"Who is the leader here?" I asked the question loudly, so my voice carried. I knew damn well it was Havoc, but this had the feeling of something that needed to be dealt with carefully. With the proper procedure.

To my absolute and total relief, Havoc stepped forward. "I am the Alpha of the Windrun Pack."

Shoulders and back straight, I strode toward him, feeling the weight of all the eyes in the clearing on us. Like out of one of my books, I had a feeling this would not only be ceremonial, but also binding.

I gathered my words, as if I were to write them for the dialogue of my heroine. Words had power, and they were my greatest asset and strength.

"I am the last supplicant for the hive's throne." I looked him in the eye. "The current queen rules from treachery and fear. Will you align yourself with me in ensuring she no longer rules?"

Havoc's eyes narrowed. "You would have us pit our strength against hers for your benefit?"

I shook my head. "I would have you fight for your future, as I fight for mine."

There was a shuffling of feet. Havoc looked around the clearing at his people. Above us, the snow began to fall once more, landing in my hair and on my bare shoulders though I barely felt the cold.

"No," Havoc said, "you must face this alone and prove your worth. If you become the new queen, I will gladly bind our pack to your hive once more."

Anger slashed through me, but it was driven by fear and loss of hope. I turned from Havoc, understanding that what he did, he did to protect his pack, and started walking. The werewolves on the edge of the clearing parted for me, allowing me to pass.

The snow was not deep and so while my skirts trailed out behind me, they did not slow me. I knew that at some point, the five vampire men would catch up to me. And if they did not, I would just keep on walking.

In the snow in New England? The question was my own, and I knew the answer. I would die of exposure if the temperature continued to drop. I stopped in my tracks and waited for them.

Wick reached me first. "What is wrong, Allianna?"

I spun to him, staring at him as I considered all the things I could say to answer that. "Seriously? You are wondering what's wrong? Do you want the full list or an abbreviated version?"

His lips tightened, anger snapping through his dark eyes. "You think you are the only one concerned about the outcome of tomorrow?"

I bit the inside of my cheek to keep from saying anything more. "I have to prepare for a fight. If you'll excuse me, I don't know the way back to the hive."

Preacher caught up to us then, though I realized they were hanging back on purpose. "You no longer want to leave with us? To have the six of us run away together?"

I stared at him, my heart hurting as I spoke. "From my mind, I cast thee."

He sucked in a sharp breath and I made myself say the rest of what I had to say. "You would not come with me if I asked, so why should I face the rejection? I understand now, Preacher. As I pointed out to you, I am no child, no girl expecting her white knight to save her. I will do what I can to save you all, whatever that takes."

Celt and King caught up, and there was no laughter between us. No soft touches. I felt used, duped by the lust and emotions that had flared between myself and all five of them. Even Spartan. He'd promised not to lie to me.

Perhaps from him I felt the most hurt in his deception. They encircled me in a protective form, and with nothing but silence between us we walked to the hive.

It took several hours, and through it all, I kept my mouth shut. To say the strain between us was heavy in the air was like saying a two-ton truck was on the large side.

Finally, the entrance to the hive opened before us.

It was not what I would have thought. A massive set of stairs made of thick steps dropped into a hollow in the ground. At the bottom of the steps, a wide set of doors stretched open. This was it, this was my last moment with any chance at freedom, of escaping this world, but even that was a pretense.

I found myself sinking onto the stairs, my skirts billowing out around me. Once I walked through those doors, there would be no leaving. I knew it.

Either I would fight and win against Terra, and four of the vampires who'd stolen my heart would die, or I would die and at least one of the vampires standing with me would die as well.

There was no way I could win this. There was no happily ever after, no fairy tale magic.

But that didn't mean I was giving up, or that I wouldn't keep fighting for them. Even if they didn't care about me. I felt too much, far too deeply for each of them to just stop trying to figure out a way around this. Really, the best I could do was win against Terra, and then demand that the old rules be cast out.

There was that continuing silence between us. Celt helped me to my feet, and then more silence as we worked our way through the narrow tunnels of the hive.

What seemed like far too soon, my bedroom door stood in front of me. I couldn't move. "Is this where the other girls were kept, too?"

Spartan nodded. "It is."

I balked. "I don't want to stay here, then. I don't care if you stick me in a closet while I wait, but I will not step foot back into a room where four women spent their last hours." With my men. That was the unspoken bit.

"You can stay in one of our rooms, lass," Celt said softly. "You know we still are with you in this."

Oh, the things I wanted to say, that I kept to myself in that moment. Like, had they been with the other girls to the end? This jealousy of mine was nothing like I'd ever felt before. Even when Mike had cheated on me, there had been no raging need to ask if the other woman was better than me, prettier, funnier.

Here, though, all I could think of was that once more I'd allowed myself to be duped by the vampires in front of me. I shook my head. "It doesn't matter to me which room."

In the end, they took me to King's room. It had the biggest bed, and nicest trappings. More suited to me, one of them said.

I stepped through the doorway and before any one of them could step through with me, I slammed it shut in their faces and threw the lock. I knew it wouldn't truly hold them back, but it was the point I was making. They were no longer allowed to hurt me. Not like this. I would save them. I knew I would.

Because I had nothing else left. I crumpled to my knees and covered my face with my hands as the tears flowed down my cheeks.

Sobbing, I couldn't seem to get control no matter how many times I reminded myself they'd fooled me. That I meant nothing to them. I needed to be the same way, to make my heart stop feeling everything it was feeling.

Because all of it had felt real and true. From Celt's laughter, to King's caress, to Preacher's need for me, to Wick's teasing, to Spartan's honesty. No, not honesty. That slowed my tears and I did all I could to hang onto the anger. It helped to keep the sobs at bay.

A knock rattled the door, and the object of my anger called out.

"Open this door, Ally, right fucking now."

I was on my feet in a flash, and I scrambled with the lock, and flung the door open wide. "Why, so you can lie to my face again?"

Spartan bared his teeth at me, fangs flashing. "I told you the truth as much as I was able."

"Bullshit!" I spit the word at him and tried to shut the door. He stuffed his foot into the doorway and I slammed the door on it.

"Son of a bitch!" he snarled, but kept his foot there, and I slammed it again.

"Get out. I don't want to talk to any of you."

"You forget something." He shoved his way into the room and threw the door shut behind him. He stalked toward me and I found myself backing up until I was against the far wall. For the first time, I was a little bit afraid of one of them.

"And just what am I forgetting?" I arched an eyebrow at him, doing my best to keep my head up and my confidence intact.

"You still owe me a fucking."

"I owe you *nothing.*" I glared at him. "And to think I would just strip down for you now when the five of you have lied to me from the beginning, when you let me believe I was someone special to you, when you didn't tell me that I was your last hope to live, and that was why you were going out of your way for me. That I was nothing but the end of a long line of whores sent to slaughter. You are out of your goddamn mind!"

My chest was heaving with the adrenaline pumping through me, my fists were clenched at my sides and my body was literally vibrating with energy and anger.

Spartan's face went from snarling to one filled with shock.

"Is that what you truly think?"

"Well, unlike you, I am actually honest when I speak my mind." I pressed against the wall, using it to hold me up because if I wasn't careful I would dissolve again once more into tears.

Spartan took a step, and then another. When I didn't protest he drew very close to me. "Shit, Ally, you could not be more wrong about what is happening here." He rubbed a hand over his face. "Will you...let me try to explain?"

I waved at him with one hand. "Be my guest. But don't expect me to fall for it again."

His shoulders slumped under the straps of his armor. "There *were* four other girls, that is the truth. Each of them chose one of our other brothers. Daemon. Prince. Hawk. Remington. They died with those women. Those women...they never touched the rest of us. They bedded one man, the strongest of us always, and ran from the rest of us."

My eyes widened. "You mean you offered to them?"

"And they turned us down. They chose one, and they died with that one."

I looked down at the hem of my skirt, hating that I was happy that those other four women hadn't touched the other brothers.

Spartan went on. "You are our last hope, but you are also the first who has embraced all of us. And I...I think that may be why you can do this. We will all stand with you. Live or die, we do it together. I cannot speak entirely for my brothers, but you are everything I have ever wanted in a woman at my side. Beauty and fire, laughter and love, a passion in your soul, and a burning lash in your tongue. We are the five youngest brothers, considered the weakest of the group, and now you have given each of us a piece of you."

There was a thump on the door and Wick called out. "He stole the words out of my mouth."

There was a second thump that made me think he'd been cuffed for saying anything. I tried not to smile at the image.

I lifted my eyes to see Spartan smile before he went on. "What I tell you now I know will not make you believe I am any more honest, but I hope you will see I am trying to make right what I've done wrong." He swallowed hard. "I was a fool, in the beginning. I thought if you died, that would save all of us."

I stared at him, his words sinking in slowly. "You were the one who knocked on the door? After my time with Wick, so he would leave. You set up the other vampire to draw me out?"

His jaw flexed and tightened. "I did. And I...I didn't think of it at the time, but I bitched at Malcom about you, and told him you were in the training arena alone."

We stared at each other, and he dropped his gaze first. I didn't know what to say.

The door behind us burst open and his four brothers were on him in a flash, tackling him to the ground. I put my fists to my mouth, torn.

He had tried to have me killed. Twice. But it was to save his brothers. Would I have done less for Dominique? I would have given anyone's life for hers. That was my job, to take care of her.

"Stop!" I yelled over the sounds of fists hitting flesh. "I said stop!"

I put my hands on Celt, the closest to me, and pulled him back, then King and Wick. Preacher was the last, holding Spartan down by the throat.

I crouched beside Preacher. "I don't know how to reverse you not being able to look in my mind, but I want you to be able to see my thoughts."

I wanted him to see I didn't blame Spartan, that I understood why he'd done what he had, and I forgave him. I wanted Preacher to see what he meant to me, what they all meant to me.

Slowly, his hands released his youngest brother. "Allianna. You cannot see in his mind."

I snorted. "Apparently neither can you, since you didn't see this coming."

Celt snickered. "Ah, she has you there, lad."

Preacher looked to me, his dark eyes full of concern. "I don't want to leave him here alone with you. It's not safe."

I touched Preacher's cheek. "What if you sat outside the door? Would that be close enough to hear our thoughts?"

He nodded. "It would. Are you sure you...still want to go through with this?"

Spartan groaned. "You say that like I'm a rutting pig that she is being forced to fuck."

Celt took a swing at Spartan with his foot. "Close enough, you idiot. She's not like the others, we tried to tell you that."

"So you did," Spartan admitted. "But I'm not known for being particularly bendable once I set my mind on something."

"Go," I stood up and waved for them to leave, then I paused. "No, actually take me back to the other room. I'm okay with being in there."

"Why is it okay now?" King asked, his green eyes meeting mine, then darting away. I smiled at him, drew close and took his hand.

"Because I thought those other four women had their way with you in that room. I couldn't bear the thought of sharing both your bodies and the beds you shared with them."

"Possessive little lass, isn't she?" Celt said, but there was no ire in his voice, more like a sense of pride. I turned and winked at him.

"Never before, but apparently, now, I have a jealous streak right up the middle of my back."

Wick grabbed me around the waist. "I think we should check that streak for infection. It could be contagious."

I squealed as he swung me over his shoulder, my voluminous skirts billowing out so wide there was no way he could see anything. Still, the five of us managed to make it back to my bedroom without tumbling. He carried me all the way into the middle of the room and the other four followed, circling around once more.

Wick set me down and I kissed him. "Thanks for the ride."

He chuckled. "Anytime."

Celt slipped in beside me, and bent me backwards over his knee for a deep tongue-tangling kiss that had me digging my hands into his hair. He pulled back only enough so that our noses touched. "Lass, Spartan be right, you are everything I ever did want in my own lassie." He let me go, handing me off to Preacher.

My quiet Preacher, so unsure in his own way, but the rock of our group. He stood a little straighter and I wrapped my arms around his waist. "Thank you."

"For what?"

I looked up at him, and he bent his head so I could whisper in his ear. "For loving me."

He closed his eyes. "You are not supposed to be able to read minds."

I shrugged. "I'm a woman of many talents."

Next was King, and he turned his face from me, cutting through the joy that was slowly blooming. "I'm sorry, King. I'm sorry I turned from you in the woods. I was so hurt, I thought...well, I thought I was just a pawn to you."

His eyes whipped back to me. "Allianna, that couldn't be further from the truth."

I lifted a shoulder. "I know that now, but I didn't then and I was trying to protect what was left of my heart."

I tipped my head and he took the invitation, planting his lips on mine, gentle and sweet and every bit my King.

I stepped back from the other four. "I trust Spartan. You can stay at the door if you like, but I trust him."

"Why?" Spartan asked the question before the others could leave. "Why do you trust me after all I've done?"

I looked him straight in the eye. "Because it is exactly what I would have done to save those I loved."

Chapter Seventeen

My words filled the air of the bedroom. I looked at each of the men. "I would have done the same to protect my sister. That is family, that is love, that is just the way it is. I understand you, Spartan, maybe because I see so much of myself in you."

"Except for the whole cock and armor bit," Wick offered.

"You think I was hiding a cock between my legs?" I grinned and arched an eyebrow at him.

Wick laughed. "The only cock that I saw there at the time was mine. But to be fair, I was so lost in you, I didn't notice much except how good it felt."

His words seemed to ignite a firestorm in my belly, reminding me of how much pleasure had already ridden in this room between me and the first four brothers, and that there was more to come. The brothers all took a step forward at once and I held my hand up.

"Hang on. I am game for a...what would that be, a six-way?" I looked to Preacher for help, and he shrugged, a pull of his lips curling into a grin.

"You'd be willing to bed all of us at the same time?" he asked.

"Would all of you be willing?" I looked around, surprised to see them all nod in rapid-fire agreement, even Spartan.

Now that would be a fuck-fest of epic proportions. Preacher coughed and looked away. "That it would be."

"To answer you," I said, "I would be willing, but not until I've had Spartan to myself." I might have blushed, more than a little with those words, which was ridiculous after all I'd done with them. But blush, I did.

I blushed and the others' laughter surrounded me as they filed out.

"Another time, and we will see who lasts the longest then," Celt said, saluting me as he closed the doors behind them.

I slowly turned to Spartan. His burnished gold eyes were locked on me. "I've wanted you from the beginning. I hated myself for wanting you."

"Well, I am irresistible." I grinned and then looked down at the dress. "I hate to ask you, but there is no way I'm getting out of this on my own."

I looked over my shoulder at the intricate lacing down the back of the corset top. "It's too nice to just tear off so don't even think about it." I looked back at him in time to see a knife in his hand as he stepped toward me.

"What about cutting it off?"

I rolled my eyes and twisted so my back faced him. "I suppose the laces can be replaced."

From the other side of the door, King hollered, "Do not cut those ties!"

Spartan laughed quietly and I joined him. "You heard the boss, get to untying."

He slid the knife into its sheath at his waist and closed the distance between us. Contrary to what he seemed to think, his fingers were deft at loosening the ties, and pulling them through the loops until the dress ballooned around me. I pushed it down, forgetting that he was behind me and that I had zero underclothes on, and only the tall red leather boots.

He ran a hand from my lower back downward over my ass cheek. I swallowed with difficulty and turned so I could see him over my shoulder. He looked at me, his eyes dilating as he slipped his other hand over the other cheek.

My pussy tightened with a speed that made me gasp. I made myself step out of the dress. There was something I had wanted to do with him since I'd first seen his body covered in dirt and sweat.

"Wait here." I pointed at his feet, and left him standing there, a look of confusion on his face. I hurried to the bathroom and went straight to the giant tub. I flicked on the water, testing the temperature and then set it to filling. I found some bubble bath that smelled like fresh cotton sheets off the line, and poured a healthy amount in while the water frothed it into a cocoon of bubbles.

I went back to the doorway and peered out at Spartan. We should have been training, but we all knew no amount of training would make up the difference between Terra and me, not at this point. We might as well enjoy the time we had left to us.

I crooked a finger at him and he stepped toward me, his eyes narrowing. I put a hand on his chest, sliding it under the thick leather bands. "Do you need help taking this off?"

He shrugged out of it, leaving him only in the metal banded kilt armor. Though kilt wasn't the right word. I wasn't about to ask him what was. I was on a mission to get it off, not get a history lesson on what it was called.

I had a giant tub filling with hot water and bubbles, and a Spartan in front of me that I had craved from the moment I'd met him.

"You know we've never even kissed?" I looked up at him. The sensation of being engulfed by his body was sudden and caught me off guard. He was broader than the other men, both in shoulders and in every aspect of his limbs. Next to him I felt petite, and more feminine than in my whole life.

"We should fix that then," he said, dipping his head. He paused when our mouths were hovering above one another, a breath apart. I flicked my tongue out and ran it over his bottom lip, to the corner of his mouth. His tongue met mine, tangling in midair before we closed the gap between us. His mouth was hot, and tasted of fire, as though I could breathe him in and he would sear my insides, branding me as his own.

I groaned into his mouth and my hands went to his belly, running my fingers across his rippled abs, over his pecs, and around his broad shoulders.

His hands made their own exploration of my body, starting in the reverse at my shoulders and making their way south. Over my arms, grazing along my breasts, sliding over my hips and brushing over the front of my pussy, then back up over my body.

I leaned into him, his armor cold against the bare skin of my hips and thighs, giving me a delicious thrill. His hands swept around to my back, caught me by either side of my ass, and pulled me tightly to him. My breasts pressed into his hard chest, and with effort, I untangled my mouth from his long enough to catch a breath.

"Armor should come off now, yes?"

"Yes," he growled, stepping back from me, unlatching what was left of his armor, flinging it to the side.

I put a hand out, stopping him from drawing me close. "I want to see all of you."

I let my eyes lower, over his chest, abs, to the straining cock that all but begged me to touch it. Lower, over his thighs and then back up, all the way to his face. "Better than I imagined even. That's saying something considering my day job."

I crooked my finger at him, turning the tables on him. He didn't step forward, but stepped and dropped to his knees. He buried his mouth in my pussy, parting the folds with a vehemence that made me gasp and dig my hands into his hair to hold myself upright. Rolling heat rushed upward through my body, sending me into a world of pleasure I thought I knew. I didn't know it like this, though, or with this man.

His tongue flicked across my clit, drawing it out enough that he could catch the nub with his lips and suckle it. A groan slid from me as the curling pleasure uncoiled through my lower regions and through the rest of me. I was on my tiptoes to help give him access, aching to press my pussy harder against him, and he took full advantage.

He continued to suckle my clit, tugging at it carefully, the gasping need in me growing with each pulse of his mouth and tongue. This, this wave of pleasure was all I wanted, and with Spartan it had been a long time coming.

With one arm, he steadied me; the other hand was free, and he slid it between my legs, finding my very wet, and very wanting pussy.

"Yes, Spartan, please, yes, fuck me," I whimpered, barely able to speak over the sensations rocketing through me. His mouth continued the steady pulse and pull on my clit, taking me to the edge of orgasm and then he'd back off, then to the edge once more we'd go.

Good God, I was going to explode with the want in my body, with what he was doing to me.

"Spartan, please!"

He didn't change tactics, just continued as if I hadn't begged him to let me come. His mouth suckled on my throbbing clit, and as I began to climb that crest once more, his fingers crept up the inside of my thighs. He set two fingers at the outer lips of my dripping core. My breath came in hitches as my body began to come to a climax that would not be denied.

"Don't stop, don't stop!"

His mouth picked up pace, and as I began to crest, he thrust his fingers into me, in and out, in time with his mouth. I arced back as the scream left me, my body cascading with an orgasm so strong, I think I might have passed out for a moment. The world swam and if not for his arm around my ass, I know I would have been flat on the floor.

My entire body shook and my legs were complete jelly. I slumped, my breathing out of sync as I slid down his arms so that we were face to face. I kissed him, tasting my moisture on his lips, my pleasure in his mouth.

He kissed me back. "Good?"

"Do you really have to ask?" I murmured into his mouth. "I can't even stand."

He grinned. "Tub?"

"Yes." I might have nodded but I was still feeling the effects of the orgasm aftershocks. Like a massive earth-quake, the tremors still rippled outward, making me twitch and jump in odd ways.

He scooped me up in his arms and carried me to the tub. His cock brushed against my backside. "You didn't get to have any fun yet."

Spartan laughed softly. "Trust me, that was fun."

I frowned, a thought flickering through me. "You boys aren't sharing crib notes, are you?"

His eyes mock widened. "What? To figure out your hot buttons so we can bring you to a screaming orgasm every single time we touch you? *Why* would we do that?"

The sarcasm was not lost on me, or the reality that it was actually pretty damn smart. I bobbed my head. "Point taken. But it means it's five against one. I am going to need a head start on learning all of your wants and desires."

Carefully, he lowered me into the tub. The hot water slid up over my limbs like another lover's caress and I let out a low hiss as the water kissed my wounded shoulder. I touched it. "This...why did it get infected?"

Spartan stepped into the tub and slid down into the water. He reached for me and towed me through the swirling warmth onto his lap. I dropped my hand, brushing it over his cock. He grunted. "You can't ask me a question and then do that."

"Sure, I can. It's called getting to the answer quickly."

He leaned back and let out a slow breath as I caressed his length, from shaft to tip.

"The wound?" I prompted.

"Malcom has a poison bite. He's from another hive and only came here because he thought he could get in good with the queen. I think."

"Hmm." I gave him a harder squeeze, then shifted my hand lower, to cup his balls, rolling them between my thumb and forefinger. He arched his back and spread his legs.

"Yeah, that's a good spot."

I leaned in and kissed him while I stroked his balls. He groaned softly, his golden eyes locked on mine.

"I hope you can forgive me," he said. "For everything."

"Already done, Spartan." I bit his upper lip in tiny nibbles, sliding my way to one of his fangs. "Besides, a little torture is good for the soul and for penance."

He opened his mouth to speak and I sucked one whole fang into my mouth, treating it to the same loving care that he'd given my clit. I wrapped it with my tongue and suckled hard on the ivory length.

A spasm rocked his body and his eyelids fluttered. I took my time caressing the fang, then slowly moved to the other and repeated the procedure, drawing it in and teasing its length.

"Enough," he breathed and adjusted me so I was straddling his lap, his cock against my pussy once more. "I want to come inside you, I want to feel your body tighten around me." He growled the words against my neck. "I fucking want all of you, Ally. Every, last, bit. Anything you'll let me have, I will take."

His hands swept up to cup my breasts, lifting them free of the water to his lips. He took a nipple into his mouth and rolled it against his teeth, tugging at the already begging piece of me. I struggled not to just slide onto his length to have him fill me up in a single thrust of his hard cock. I wanted to, but I also wanted this to last. I knew what it was, my last time with him, with any of them before I had to face the queen. I wanted as many sensations of this man as I could get in the little time we had.

His mouth moved to my other breast while his free thumb swept across the previous nipple. I couldn't stop the whimper in the back of my throat. I let myself slide down on his cock, taking him deeply into me. I took him in and then didn't move. His eyes were on mine as he let my breasts go and swept his arms around me. I wrapped my arms around his neck as tears pooled in my eyes. This moment was perfect in so many ways and to think it would be the last time killed a piece of my heart.

Spartan shifted and began to rock his hips a little. I matched his pace, and together we caused a mini wave pool in the big tub as we found a pace and rhythm that was beyond anything this side of heaven I'd ever experienced. This was where I was meant to be, my whole life had been building to these last few days. The good, the bad, all of it.

The orgasm took me by surprise and I leaned into him, kissing him as my pussy convulsed around his cock, begging him to come with me. With a cry, he followed me into the climax, his body jerking against mine, his hands digging into my back even as I bit the side of his neck, holding on for all I was worth.

The water stilled around us, and I looked up to see Preacher, King, Celt and Wick at the tub's edge. I smiled at them though it was watery and filled with tears. "What are you waiting for? You might as well come on in while the water is warm."

Chapter Eighteen

We played in the tub, the six of us, like children in a swimming pool. Well, except for the occasional tweak of a nipple, or slide of a finger into my pussy, the whole shindig was pretty straightforward fun. The reality was, I wasn't the only one feeling the pressure of what was coming and we were all handling it by ignoring it. By pretending that decision time was not drawing closer and closer. So, we played in the tub, splashing one another, the slippery water a perfect place for wrestling matches between the men. Mostly that was Celt offering to take on anyone. The others just held him under the water until he gave up.

Preacher, though, being the rock of the group, was the one to break up the tub time. "The fight will happen in a little over an hour. Allianna, I'm sorry, but you need to choose one of us."

The words fell like a giant boulder into the tub, stealing what was left of the warmth from the water. I shivered and wrapped my arms around my upper body. Celt was closest to me and he wrapped his arms around me too.

"No matter who you choose, lassie, we all will love you still."

His words started a torrent of tears. "I can't choose!"

They helped me out, all five of them touching me, drying me off, trying their best to reassure me, but they didn't understand. I literally could not choose from them. I couldn't say one over the others would be best as they all fit me, just in different ways.

"You must," Preacher said. "Because you will take your consort and face Terra and her beast of a consort. Amos is one of the few true shifters in our hive, and he is deadly."

I kept my arms clamped around my upper body. "They've killed four of your brothers. The oldest four." They shared a glance and I nodded. "I get it. Terra and Amos have already killed the four strongest of you."

Wick sighed, all the laughter in him gone. "Yes. But there is no choice. Your first bite will cement the bond."

I shuddered and then a horrible, horrible thought rocketed through me. "My...first bite?"

They all nodded and I raised my hands up to my mouth, my thoughts racing to the arena, to Malcom tackling me. Preacher paled and stumbled back.

"Mother of God," he whispered, catching onto where my mind had gone, seeing my thoughts. "I didn't even consider it."

"Consider what?" Spartan demanded. "One of you talk to us."

"Malcom bit my shoulder," I said. "He was my first bite."

Four sets of jaws dropped in perfect unison.

I was shaking so hard I couldn't stand. Malcom, that asshole Malcom was the one I had to put my life in the hands of. I closed my eyes. The men were talking fast above me but I let myself dive into my own thought. I banished Preacher from my mind, because I needed to be alone. Slowly, a plan stirred and I let out a slow breath. This was what I'd wanted, a way to save all five of the men my heart had chosen. If I failed, at least Malcom would be the one to die, not any of my men.

Cold, callous, but the truth, it was. But Malcom had a bite filled with poison, and that alone could save us. All he needed to do was get one fang into Terra, and she would die.

I raised my hand and stilled their words. "Bring me Malcom."

Spartan didn't argue, but took off still naked, grabbing his armor as he left. I looked to Preacher and let him back inside my thoughts. Slowly he nodded. "It could work, yes, it could indeed work. But you will still have the guards to deal with if it does work. They will come for us because they are under her spell."

"Then you cannot be here," I said softly. "The five of you go to the wolves."

"I will not leave you," King said, surprising me with the vehemence in his voice. "I will not!"

"It is the only choice!" I stood and stared hard at him. "If you are there, you are safe. If you are safe, I will do what I must and not be distracted by worry for you!"

Celt and Wick were shaking their heads, but it was Celt who spoke. "No, we can't do this. We won't leave you again."

I turned to him and put my hand to his cheek. "If you were to face her, and thought it was safer for me to be away, to be out of the line of fire, would you expect me to go?"

His head dropped and he closed his eyes. I glared at him. "Don't you dare say it's because I'm a woman either."

"I wasn't," he mumbled, but I saw the twist of his lips. Even in this, he could find the humor. That was what had drawn me to him, the cheeky bastard.

There was a clattering of noise in the bedroom. The four men strode ahead of me, leaving me alone for a moment in the bathroom. I thought about wrapping in a towel, but thought better of it, and just strode forward naked as the day I was born.

Malcom was on his knees with Spartan hovering over him.

"Fuck you, Spartan." He glared up at all the brothers.

I snapped my fingers at Malcom. "You are under the queen's commands, are you not?"

His blue eyes swept over my body, hunger lighting them up. "I am."

"And if you were to be in the inner circle of the queen, what would that be worth to you?"

His eyes widened. "What are you saying?"

I crouched in front of him, being sure to keep my knees closed tightly. "I *am* going to be queen, Malcom. You can choose to help me now, or you can choose to continue to piss me off to the point that the empty cage in the lower basement will look like a goddamn palace to you by the time I'm done with your sorry ass."

The men shifted around me. I stayed where I was, buck naked, and yet I'd never felt stronger and more confident in my entire life. "Either way, you are bound to me, Malcom." I wanted to call him a fucking moron, but I figured that would defeat the purpose of what I was trying to make happen here. "You are my first bite, whether either of us likes it or not."

His jaw dropped, flashing his fangs. Fangs that were not completely white like the others I'd seen, but tinged with green at the base. My jaw ticked. "Your bite is poison, even to another vampire, correct?"

He nodded. "It is."

I clasped my hands around my knees. "You are going to stand with me against the queen, and her consort, Amos. Those are the rules, and we will abide by them. But she does not need to know it will be you fighting until the last second. Do you understand?"

His eyes widened. "A sneak attack?"

I nodded.

Malcom looked from me to the other men. "How do you know I won't run to her?"

This was where things were going to get ugly. Preacher stepped forward. "I will stand next to Allianna. The queen will believe I am the one who has been chosen as the oldest of us left. I will be in your mind, Malcom. If you try to warn her, Spartan will kill you where you stand. He will be with you until the fight begins and then he will leave."

Wick, Celt, and King stiffened.

Wick shook his head. "If they are staying, we are staying." The other two nodded their agreement.

I looked to Preacher for help and he slowly shook his head. "I would fight to stay too."

I knew I'd lost this argument. I knew I had as much as I knew that if they tried to send me away from them now, I would fight to remain.

"Damn it. Fine. We are all in this. Win or lose, we are in. Malcom, are you with us then?"

He flicked his eyes over me. "Am I a part of your harem then?"

A shudder slid through me, and I tried to push the pulse of lust away, but it climbed over me. He was handsome and deadly, and I didn't trust him, but try telling my blind libido that. "Yes. But it will have to wait until after we are done with this."

"No," Spartan said. "You need him bound to you now, as we are. We all need him bound to us so we are together in this."

He took a knife from his hand and slashed it across his palm. He passed the blade around to the other men and in under a minute they had all opened their hands. The knife went to Malcom and he did the same. Malcom held out his hand and the others squeezed their blood into his palm. His eyes drifted closed and he let out a slow breath. "I am with you, come what may. I am with you. I am part of this fist."

I didn't trust him enough to be alone with him. I looked at Preacher and the others. "Will you stay? Please?"

They nodded and moved away from where Malcom knelt. With each of the men I'd bedded, I'd found a reason to connect with them, a missing piece of my heart, and I wasn't sure I could do it with Malcom. We'd started out on the wrong foot, or the wrong foot in the balls to be exact.

"Not how I thought we'd end up," I said.

He grunted and rolled his eyes. "Yeah. But I'll admit, you intrigued me even then."

"Why?" I needed to get the words out, to see if there was something we could build from.

The lines between his brows deepened. "Being able to deny me, even while you were still human, is supposed to be impossible. Impossible is a word I don't like."

"Can I touch you?" I asked. "I want to see if that heat that was there in the beginning still is now."

He gave me the barest of nods.

I slowly reached out and touched Malcom's cheek.

He held still, as if he expected a blow over a gentle touch. I bit my lower lip. "Who hurt you?"

He turned his face away. "No talking."

The other men laughed, the sound rolling around the room. "Good luck with that," Wick grumbled. I shot him a dirty look. He winked back at me.

Malcom slid out of his coat, and shed his shirt. "If we are doing this, then we are doing it now."

It was only then I realized he *didn't* want to do this, he didn't want to be with me despite the pull between us.

I took a step back. "I won't force you, Malcom. That is not my way."

He closed his eyes and a sigh slid out of him. "Damn you. That is not how this works. It just is this way, and we are fucking."

I took another step back and he lunged for me, snagging me around the thighs and pulling me down so my body was under his, flat on the floor. The scene from the training room flooded me and Preacher was there in a flash at my side, one hand on my shoulder, the other on Malcom's.

"Easy, Malcom. Easy. Her memories of you are not pleasant no matter how strong the call to your flesh is for her."

Malcom held still and I got my heartbeat back under control. I looked up at Preacher.

"Thank you. I'm...I'm okay now."

Malcom bent his head and then moved so his lips were away from mine. He shook his head. "My kiss and bite are poison. Vampires like me are not supposed to have bonds like this. We are born to be loners."

Those words held a great deal of pain, and for a moment I thought I saw a flicker of his past in his eyes. Treated badly, tortured, made to do things he didn't want. This man was not the shithead I'd thought.

He'd been acting on orders he couldn't deny.

I snorted. "Look, it isn't like I want a repeat of the bite, but you are here, and you are part of our..." I paused, uncertain of what to truly call what this was. More than a harem of men, that was for sure. Family...that was the word, but it was strange sounding when there was just little old me with six men at my beck and call.

Preacher laughed softly. "Family is as good a word as any, Allianna. Far better than consorts or harem."

Malcom was staring at me with those summer-blue eyes of his. "You consider this family?"

I lifted a shoulder. "I don't know what else to call it. Family is more than love. It is loyalty, it is laughter, it is light and dark, forgiveness and hope for the future." I dared to touch his face, cupping it with the palm of my hand. "It is being open to possibilities and taking them for what they are."

He frowned, closed his eyes and swallowed hard enough that it was audible. "And what is this then?"

"Fate. You found me, and you brought me here, which means from the beginning you've been a part of my journey into this world. A world I am willing to fight for now." The words seemed to pour out of me, filling the space between us and softening the antagonism there from the beginning.

"I didn't want...to hurt you on the field." He leaned his head against my shoulder. "Preacher, am I being honest?"

Preacher answered him. "You are. Terra controlled you. She can't now, your bond is to Allianna."

Malcom shuddered.

I gave him a gentle tap on the shoulder. "When this is done, when I am queen, I will make you an offer."

His eyes swept to mine. "What kind of offer?"

"I will give you a choice. You can stay with me, bound to me, or you can go, and live your life however you want."

"Not possible," Preacher said.

I didn't look at him. "Anything is possible when you stop believing it isn't."

The other men didn't argue with me, and I wasn't sure if they were just humoring me or making it so Malcom would help.

Malcom nodded. "A choice, something I have not had in all my years."

"You going to fuck her?" Celt barked out. "Because if not, then we need to get going."

I locked eyes with Malcom. "Up to you."

He shook his head. "I want all my energy for the fight. I want to win, not have my head handed to me and shoved into the sunlight."

I smiled, leaned forward and kissed his cheek. "Good. So, do I."

He raised himself off me and offered his hand. I took it and he helped me to stand. The coursing lust for his skin was still there, but it had tempered, and obviously, he'd managed to master it as well.

"To war we go." I looked around the room at the men with me. I would choose them all if I could. As it was...my choice had been made for me. For all of us.

I rested my eyes on Malcom.

He nodded and straightened his shoulders. "To battle, to hope for the future."

I lifted a hand, fisted to him, and he knocked his fisted hand on mine. "Boom goes the new queen."

Chapter Nineteen

King helped me dress while Celt and Wick argued over what I should wear.

"The black catsuit, I think that is fitting," I pointed out. "And it's easy to move about in."

King agreed quietly. His hands shook as he laced up a black corset over the suit. "This will give you some extra protection from the blows."

I drew a breath in, held it and slowly let it out, doing what I could to calm my nerves. It was only in that moment of quiet that I remembered the tiny container that Ralph had given me. "Spartan, would you check the red dress for a flask? It's not very big, but I think I dropped it when we came in here."

Wick snickered. "Had other things on your mind, did you?"

I grinned and winked at him. "You bet."

Spartan rummaged through the voluminous skirts. "Are you sure?"

My mouth went dry. That flask could be the difference between surviving and finding myself drained completely. "Shit."

Our walk from the Windrun pack had been anything but comfortable. I'd been furious. Could I have dropped the flask? I'd not even thought of it until just now.

"What was it?" Malcom asked. "A nip of whiskey I can get you if that's all it was."

I shook my head. "Essence of Lillianna."

All six heads swiveled toward me. "What did you say?" Celt was the first to break the silence.

"Ralph gave it to me. He said that it would help me channel Lillianna, that she'd been a great fighter and that she'd only lost to Terra because of trickery." I looked into their faces, hoping Ralph had not been lying to me. Spartan was the one who answered my unspoken questions.

"It is possible. I didn't think Ralph and Lily were that close. I'll check the stairs, and start back tracking through the forest. Hold off as long as you can." He darted close to me, planted his lips on mine, the prick of his fangs as he pressed them tightly to my lips. He whispered against them, "I love you, Ally."

Then he was gone in a blur. I stood in the middle of the room, feeling the minutes tick by on my skin, a tightening sensation I couldn't escape.

"How long?" I asked.

"Fifteen minutes," King said.

The amount of energy flowing through me did not want to be contained. I needed to move, run, something, anything.

In my mind, I could see the fight play out, as if I were writing a scene in a book. I would face Terra with

Preacher at my side. As the oldest, he was the most reasonable one for me to have chosen. The other men would hang back, far enough that if I failed, they would have a chance to get away before they were taken to slaughter.

I knew they wouldn't, though, and that thought gutted me. If I failed and lost to Terra, I knew the others would rush to my side. I knew they would go down with me. I clenched my hands into fists, then spread my fingers wide over and over. Malcom touched my arm.

"Two minutes."

I bit my lower lip and nodded. Though I had to force myself, I ran through the few moves Spartan had taught me. But I was slow, human slow, and I fumbled even those simple moves, with my nerves getting the better of me.

I was so afraid that without Lillianna's essence, I would be sunk. I pressed the heels of my hands into my eyes and counted down the last sixty seconds in my head.

They ticked by incredibly fast and before I knew it I was at ten, nine, eight, seven, six, five, four, three, two, "One," I whispered.

No more delaying this, no more thinking about how to win this fight. I squared my shoulders and started toward the door, Preacher at my side. The other three fell in behind us. I found Preacher's hand as we walked the narrow hallway. My hand was clammy, damp with nerves and the clear understanding I was walking to my death.

Try and get them out, when I lose to her, please try and get you and the others out. I can't bear to think of all of you dying because I am not strong enough. My thoughts were clear, directed at Preacher to make sure he heard them.

His hand tightened on mine. I hoped he did as I asked.

The narrow hallways opened as we moved past the hospital rooms, past the training room and to a place I'd not been before.

"This is the arena," Preacher said. "It is only used when a queen is challenged for her throne."

"Sounds peachy keen," I muttered. "The blood of the losers saturates the ground, and their souls cry out for revenge."

Malcom snorted. "Waxing poetic, are we?"

"Writer brain." I tapped the side of my head. "Can't help it sometimes."

As Preacher and I stepped into the arena, I got a good look at the place. Not so unlike the training field, it was smaller in size, only about as big around as an ice rink.

Unlike the training ground, though, the footing was not smooth turf, but shattered and broken as though bombs had been dropped and huge craters had developed as a result. Some of the craters held pools of dark water.

I wrinkled up my nose at the thought of the water stagnant for a thousand years.

"Not quite that long," Preacher said, "but close. I wouldn't get into it if you don't have to. The stink is damn hard to get off. Hawk threw me in once, I stunk for three weeks."

I knew what he was doing, distracting me, and I appreciated it, but also understood we had to focus.

Malcom was an unknown, and I was placing my life, and the lives of the men I loved, in his hands. Terrifying as that was, I had to face Terra and her consort, Amos.

"Amos, what can you tell me about him?" I queried softly. I cursed myself. I should have asked sooner.

"He's one of the few vampires able to truly change shape. His preference is for a large snouted lizard that walks on two legs."

My lips twitched and a nervous giggle escaped me. "You mean like Godzilla?"

Preacher grinned as he shook his head. "Not as big, but yes, similar enough."

I laughed, I couldn't help it. It was too fucking funny. "No wonder she keeps winning."

Again, he smiled at me. "Even now, you find joy, Allianna. That is why you must win. You will change our world for the better."

I went to my tiptoes and kissed him, not caring others were watching, not caring that the arena was surrounded by those who would try and kill my lovers if I won, and would try to kill me if I lost.

"Ahh, how sweet, they're *in love*," Terra the Twat called out, giving us an exaggerated clap of her hands. "Wonderful, now let's get on with this. I have a dinner waiting for me." She snapped her fingers and from behind her was dragged a figure I knew all too well.

I stared at the dark hair and flashing green eyes of my best friend. I took a step before I could catch myself. "Cassie!"

Cassie tried to lift her head but it was forced back down by the vampire holding her. I shook my head.

"You twinky bitch, you think that will help your cause? You think that—"

"And dessert." Terra snapped her fingers and my heart plummeted. Literally dropped out of my chest as Dominique was shoved into the light. Her blue-green eyes stared at me, but there was not one tear. Her face was a hard sight, and within seconds I knew that mine reflected the anger and fury in my little sister's.

One did not mess with the Swift sisters and get away with it.

"Wrong. Fucking. Move. Bitch." I didn't wait for anyone to tell me it was time. I didn't wait for someone to ring a bell. I rushed Terra, tapping into everything that made me who I was. Joy. Rage. Laughter. Loyalty.

Terra's eyes widened as I bodily slammed into her. I didn't go for finesse. I had none. I tackled her as if we were out playing football. We slammed onto the ground while the crowd around us roared their approval.

She let out a screech and swung a fist at my face. I ducked down close, and her fist sailed over my head. There was a roar of a beast, and I knew Amos was coming. I had a very short time to make this my stand, and to make it count.

Fast, I had to end this before it truly started.

I wrapped my hands around Terra's neck and dug my fingers in, squeezing for all I was worth. I didn't dare take my eyes off her face.

She dug her hands into my arms scratching and clawing at me, drawing blood in long rakes that made me hiss. But I was not letting go. She'd stolen my sister, and the bitch queen was going to die. I was saving my men. I was saving Cassie.

I was saving my sister. A burst of energy ripped through me and I redoubled my hold on her.

"Ally, look out!" Malcom gave me the warning, a split second too late.

There was a glimmer of thick dark-scaled skin and then it was like I'd been hit by a Mack truck. Terra's consort rammed into me, throwing me off the twat and sending me sailing through the air, ass over teakettle.

Before I even slowed my rolling, I scrambled to get to my feet. My mind was in a haze of rage I'd never experienced, and I could no longer control myself. Amos indeed looked like Godzilla, though on a seven-foot scale rather than seventy. I ran toward him. "Come on, mofo, let's do this."

It was like every fight scene I'd ever written had come back to me, every battle, every time my heroines had to take a stand. I channeled my characters into my movement, letting it guide me.

At the last second of my run, as his meaty big clawed fists swept toward me, I dropped to the ground and slid between his legs. As I passed his rather large and wrinkled ball sack, I shot a hand up and grabbed it for all I was worth.

His roar turned into a screech of agony that scaled from a low C to a high A in rapid pace. I stood behind him, his balls crushed in my hands as I looked around for the queen.

She stood facing Preacher, a *sword* in her hands, the tip pressed against his chest. "Let him go, or your mate dies."

Behind her, Malcom crept closer, his fangs exposed. How long before someone in the crowd shouted out? Did we have time?

"Did you hear me?" Terra sneered, her young-looking face twisted with...fear.

I raised myself upright but did not loosen my hold on the consort. He was bent over at the waist now, struggling to breathe. "Can't do much fucking if I rip his balls and dick off."

Her eyes narrowed and Amos whimpered, "Please, Terra, let her win. We will leave, we still have each other."

"Rip them off for all I care," she snapped. "He was never any good at fucking anyway."

Amos roared, "You traitorous whore!"

She grinned at me. "See? He's only good for fighting. It's why I chose him. You...I'm surprised you didn't choose Spartan. He at least could have put up a good fight. Preacher here, he's the oldest, but he was never the fighter of the group."

I let Amos's balls go. "You can kill her if you like. Won't bother any of us none."

He shifted as he fell away from me, down to his knees. I didn't turn my back on him, but turned so I could keep them both in my sight.

Malcom was almost to her. Almost.

His eyes shot to mine and I nodded. Terra saw it, spun and swept the sword up. Preacher caught her arms and pinned them to her sides, but not fast enough.

Malcom caught the blade across his belly, opening him up like a can of spaghetti 0's.

He went down. I was running, Spartan was yelling something from the distance.

I didn't slow, but ran harder, knowing there wasn't much time with an injury like that. "Hold her, Preacher!"

"I've got her. She cannot sway me," Preacher said. I was on my knees in a flash, doing what I could to help Malcom hold his intestines in place.

"What can I do?"

"You can't do anything." His breathing was ragged. "It's not like the movies, we die just like you die."

I looked back to Preacher. "Will blood help?"

"It will, but his bite would wound you again, and I don't know that we could get you to the pack in time." Preacher shook his head. "You cannot chance it, my queen."

Terra screamed. "I am not beaten!"

I took the sword from the ground and drove it into her belly, stopping before it pierced her back. "You are now, twat."

Preacher let her go and she slumped forward. I grabbed her by the hair and dragged her to Malcom. "I know she's a shit quality of blood, but will it help?"

He took her by the face and yanked her to his mouth, burying his fangs into her neck. She screamed, but the scream faded and then was gone as he drew the blood from her. I watched as his stomach healed before my eyes, until the wound was gone and his flesh smooth once more if still covered in blood.

I smiled at him even though the edges of it wobbled. "We did it."

The vampires around us shifted, like the motion of a wave rolling out into the ocean so it could pick up speed and send a tsunami into shore. I didn't like how this was feeling.

I stood and did a slow circle as a dozen vampires began to close ranks around us. They wore armor and had swords like Terra's. I swallowed hard.

Every sword was pointed at us. Or more specifically... Me.

Chapter Twenty

All my men, including Malcom, circled around me, facing outward to the attackers. Bare-handed. I knew there would be massive wounds, and not enough blood donors to heal them all.

"NO!" I shouted the word and there was...a click inside my head like a puzzle piece falling into the final missing spot.

"To your knees!" Again, the command was shouted, but more than that, it came with a power that welled from my belly upward.

My men dropped first, each of them to one knee. Then outward the kneeling went, as the other vampires dropped one at a time, including those with swords.

"There will be no more death." I turned a slow circle as I spoke, letting my hands touch my men one at a time.

Preacher.

Wick.

King.

Celt.

Spartan.

Malcom.

Six men, bound to me and making me whole in ways I'd never understood was possible before. "There will be no more death, as long as I am queen."

One of the vampires pushed to his feet, pointing a sword in my direction. I glared at him and he lowered the tip, but still spoke. "Our rules are set. Those you have not chosen must die."

"Rules are made to be broken," I said.

"You can't love more than one," he snarled, and took a step forward.

I flung my hand at him, palm out. "Do not!"

But it was too late, his momentum and anger swelled upward and seemed to spill into the rest of the vampires, the last of Terra clinging to them.

How did I stop this? Already my hold on them slipped, the power in my words faded with the rage Terra had left them with. I saw that now, they fed on their queen's emotions. Her stability became the hive's.

Terra had been filled with fury and cruelty.

The last vestiges of it were now facing me.

As the other vampires stalked toward us, I drew my breath to speak.

A long, echoing howl rolled through the arena, stilling every foot. A rush of winter wind, and then the arena was flooded with a pack of giant werewolves that circled around me and my men.

Havoc was there, looking far better than when I'd seen him last in his wolf form. His fur was no longer matted, his ribs no longer showed, and he didn't stink like shit and death. A decided improvement.

Our eyes met, and I gave him a nod.

"Our allies stand with me," I said softly. "A war between us and the Windrun pack would result in much death."

I bit my lower lip, wanting the right words, the ones that would make them understand. But how to make them understand what love was, and the power of it?

Spartan held something out to me.

Essence of Lillianna.

She'd been the queen that all had loved. I moved to take it, to take whatever help she would give me.

No, this had to be all me, or not at all. They would never trust in me fully if I let Lillianna have her speech now in this pivotal moment. My words would sway them, or none at all would.

I dropped my hand, not taking the bottle. "This world," I said, stepping between my men and standing between the ranks of the werewolves, "it is too dark a place to fill it with more anger. Friendship, love, laughter, these are what I bring to you. I bring you an era of peace, of loyalty, and freedom." I made my way past the circle of the werewolves to the other vampires.

To my vampires.

I walked straight to the one who had challenged me. "I give you freedom. I give you the choice to stay or go." He blinked at me, like I'd spoken a foreign language.

"Why would you do this?"

"Find your passion, find your love, find your joy." I reached up and touched his face, cupping his cheek gently. "That is what I want for all of you."

The tension in the room spiked, and I realized that this moment would tell me whether we lived or died. The fight with Terra was nothing to this. This moment would define whether I would truly be the queen, or I would have to fight once more for my life, and pray my men survived too.

He slowly went to both knees, his eyes never leaving mine.

"My queen, I have waited all my life for you."

I kissed him on the forehead, gently. "I'm sorry I took so long."

He barked a laugh and shook his head. "We have been under Terra's thumb for too long. We will have to learn to trust our queen again."

I helped him stand and then went back to my men, my throat tightening as I did so.

I looked each of them in the eye and spoke softly. "I will give each of you the same choice. Stay, if you wish to stay with me, and go, if you wish to go."

One by one they dropped to a knee and bowed their heads to me. Until Malcom. I smiled at him.

"It's okay, Malcom. Do what your heart tells you."

His shoulders tightened and flexed and he looked to the ceiling before slowly backing away. "Freedom is not something I've ever had, and I will never forget you, Allianna. Thank you."

I bowed my head to him, strangely sad that he would not stay. But I understood. This was not his place, this was not his story.

"You will always have a place here, if you wish it."

He grinned at me. "Perhaps one day I will, but not today."

With that he turned and was gone, disappearing into the crowd.

After that, things got a little...chaotic, to say the least.

If I'd ever wondered what a bunch of drunken were-wolves and vampires looked like as they ushered in a new era, I had that answer shortly after Malcom left.

The werewolves had brought a drink that contained alcohol and blood, and they freely shared it with the vampires, including my men.

I made my way through the crowd to Cassie and Dominique, who held back, and I didn't blame them. Cassie's eyes rested on Havoc more than once, and I wondered if that was a good or a bad thing. Remembering the dream I'd had of her surrounded by werewolves, I suspected her journey was just starting.

I grabbed Dominique first, dragging her into a hug. Even though she was only a couple of years younger than me, she was, and always would be, my baby sister.

"Ally?" She hugged me tightly.

"Yeah?"

"You were seriously bad-ass out there. Remind me not to get into a fight with you."

I laughed and kissed the side of her head. "I was so fucking mad they'd snatched you."

Her eyes so like my own blinked several times as if she didn't comprehend. "You...you did that because of me?"

"Hell, yeah. Nobody messes with a Swift and gets away with it, you know that." I hugged her a little tighter. "Dominique...have you been having dreams?"

She stiffened and pulled away from me. "No."

Nothing else, just no, so I guessed that meant yes. "Just don't worry when weird shit starts happening. I think it's supposed to. I think this is the world where we belong."

"You're taking this all rather well." Cassie had both eyebrows high.

I shrugged. "I wrote about it for years. If I'm dead, then this is my heaven. And if I'm alive, this is the best life I could have imagined."

Cassie laughed. "Of course, you would get my fantasy, wouldn't you?"

Her eyes drifted to Havoc and I leaned in close to her ear. "Thinking of doing it doggy style, are you?"

"Damn straight." She flashed me a smile and I couldn't help the laugh.

"Honey, just make sure he doesn't bite you, or you're going to need stock in Bic razors."

I linked arms with them both and drew them into the crowd. "Come on, I want you to meet the five men who stole my heart."

"FIVE?" Dominique bellowed, and I grinned at her.

"Well, there could have been a sixth, but I let him go." I gave her a wink and she just gaped at me. I couldn't blame her. A week ago, I would have been shocked about two men and one woman, never mind five.

Now, here I was introducing those five men to my baby sister while she blushed and stammered, and to my best friend Cassie while she...kept looking for Havoc. He was in trouble if she'd set her sights on him.

Preacher met my eyes and nodded his agreement.

"Do I have to be here? Like do I have to be sworn in or some official shit like that?" I asked the men, and they all shook their heads in tandem.

"Nah, lassie, this is it." Celt took my hand and kissed it. "You beat Terra, you claimed us all and calmed the masses. Let us play with the puppies. You take those pretty lassies back to your room and talk about makeup and boys." He grinned and I gave him a mock shove on his shoulder.

"What do you want me to do, rate the five of you?"

The shocked looks on their faces were priceless, so I took that as our cue to leave.

Cassie and Dominique walked with me back to my room.

We did indeed talk about men, sex, and all manner of things except that which we probably should have talked about. What would happen now? I was queen of the vampires. Where did that leave me?

I slapped my hand to my forehead. "Shit, I didn't meet the deadline on that last book."

Cassie shrugged. "Does it matter?"

"Yeah," I said, "to me, it does. Maybe I'm not going back to being a writer, but I can't leave my readers hanging. I just can't be *that* author."

"How long will it take?" Dominique asked as she slid her hands through my hair, braiding it into tiny sections.

"A couple of hours at most. I just had to wrap up the last of the edits and send it off to my publisher."

"Then we can do it tomorrow," Dominique said.

"A day trip," Cassie said.

"And then back to the pack?" I lifted an eyebrow at her. She rolled her eyes.

"Well, duh."

A few minutes later, Cassie was snoring, leaving me and Dominique time to talk sister to sister.

"Dominique, you are handling all of this really well, too."

She shrugged. "After reading all your stories for all these years, this doesn't seem all that weird."

I put my hands on hers. "You know that no matter what happens, I will always look out for you."

She tightened her fingers around mine. "Yeah, I know."

Time to tell her what I'd seen in my dream. Just in case it was real. "I had a dream about you and there was magic all around you, Dominique. Magic and more than a few men. I think...just be safe, and—" I couldn't get the words out because I wanted to tell her to always come back to me, but I didn't think that would happen. Not this time.

My baby sister was going to grow up finally.

Her eyes were on mine. "I know. I've been running from them a long time. I...I am going to face them down."

I blinked at her. "Face who down?"

"The men who call to me in my dreams," she said. "They call to me. It's why—"

"Why you sleep so much." I nodded. "Okay. If you need me, you know where I am, right?"

She hugged me to her. "I know where you are, where you've always belonged and where you are finally treated like the queen you are."

Chapter Twenty-One

"THE END." I typed the last words to what would be my last book, at least for a while. I had a whole hive to take care of, clean up, and make room for all the newcomers. Word of my succession had spread, and vampires were asking to come into our hive from all over the world. Most interesting were the female vampires from the few hives run by a single king.

They were beautiful, but so very broken. I wasn't sure that coming into our hive where the men were yet learning to throw off the violence and anger that was Terra's influence was a good idea. But I was willing to meet with them.

A large pair of hands kneaded into my shoulders. "This is a lovely house you live in, lass," Celt said, nipping at the top of my ear.

I leaned back into him, and hit send on the email that held my final manuscript.

"It is."

"With a rather large bed for a single woman," he pointed out. He'd been snooping, had he?

Celt was the only one to come with me to my house. Not because the others didn't want to come, but because they'd drawn straws. There was much to be done at the hive to make it a better place, and that started right away. Which meant we couldn't spare more than one guard.

The moonlight flickered in around us and I shook my head. "We have a few hours before we have to be back to the hive. Do you want an official tour of the house?"

Celt's hands tightened on my shoulders. "Yes, I'd like to test that bed out."

I took his hand from my shoulders and led him out of the office and up the wide staircase. I pushed the double doors to my bedroom open and swept a hand outward. "The bed." I took a running leap and jumped into the middle of it.

Though there had been no blood exchange, I was gaining the power and the strength of a vampire. According to Preacher, that was a result of besting Terra. The magic conferred upon me all the strength and power a queen would need.

Boo-ya for me.

Celt leapt onto the bed and we bounced around like kids, putting the bedsprings to the test for sure. From the floor, my husky dog, Luke, watched with concerned eyes.

In mid-jump, Celt caught me and dragged me to him. "I believe I owe you an orgasm or two."

"I'll take two, thank you very much." I leaned into him. "And maybe I'll let you have one?"

"Ah, my queen is too kind."

He kissed me, his lips hot and hard against mine, his mouth tasting of one piece of my heaven. I had my hands under his shirt and was stripping it off, breaking the kiss only to get the shirt off his head. After that, clothes flung in every direction until we were naked, our skin flush against one another, hot and full of need.

His hands trailed over my skin. "I want every inch of you, lassie."

"I don't think we have quite that much time," I murmured as his mouth began a wicked trail from my throat over my chest and to my nipples. He sucked the first one into his hot, wet mouth and dragged on it, holding it between his teeth and flicking the tip over and over. I arched my hips, wanting to feel his cock inside me. I might have even said that out loud, I'm not sure. All I know is that I wanted to be royally fucked.

I laughed at my own pun, and Celt glanced up at me. "What is it, lass?"

I shook my head as he slid the tip of his cock over my clit, rubbing it with his hardness, as he whispered into my ear, "Come for me, lassie, come hard and fast."

The combination of his voice and cock brought me to a screaming climax before I could answer him. The wild sensation floated through my limbs, tightening its hold on me and then slowly releasing my body until I floated back to earth.

Celt stroked my face as he slid his hard length into me. "You going to tell me what you were laughing about?"

I smiled up at him. "I can't explain it, but let's just call it writer's brain."

We made it back to the hive with plenty of time to spare before dawn. Luke came with us, of course I couldn't leave him behind. He happily trotted at my side, almost strutting like he knew we'd moved up in the world.

The quarters I'd been given as the queen were huge, easily five times the size of my previous one. I made sure they weren't giving me Terra's old room. I didn't want anything to do with that crazy bitch, even now.

Celt strutted in first. "Hello, laddies."

"Got laid, did you?" Wick shook his head and rolled his eyes.

I swatted Celt on the ass and started stripping my own clothes off. I wanted to shower, and then crawl into bed. While they assured me I didn't need to sleep, I wanted to feel that soft oblivion after all that happened. I wanted to feel my men's bodies close to me, holding me and knowing we were all safe. I wanted to be reminded that we had done the impossible and all had survived.

Surprising me, Preacher helped me shower. "Why is it surprising?"

I shrugged. "King has been the one with the deft hands for helping me. Not that your hands aren't deft, but he tends to lead in this area."

Preacher smiled down at me, his dark blue eyes full of peace now. Peace, instead of sorrow. "Come on, we have a surprise for you."

Wrapped in nothing but a towel, my hair still damp, I followed him through the suite into the bedroom.

My jaw dropped. Not only was the bed massive, easily big enough for me and my five men, they were all waiting for me. Everyone single one of them naked, every single one of them wearing a shit-eating grin on his face.

"You did say you were going to take us all for a ride, didn't you?" Preacher whispered in my ear, as his hands slid over my breasts, cupping their weight. I leaned into him, his cock hard against my ass.

"I hate to be the one to ask, but anyone know where everything is supposed to go?" I asked.

They laughed with me as I crawled into bed with them, touching and tasting as I went...my heart swelled as I let them take over, as I let them share my body, my life, and my heart. Who knew it would take five men to bring me to a love I could have never understood, could never have even dreamed of?

I closed my eyes, letting the sensations roll over me. I was their queen, they were my men, they were my everything.

And for the first time I knew I was where I belonged. I was home.

Coming July 4th, 2017...

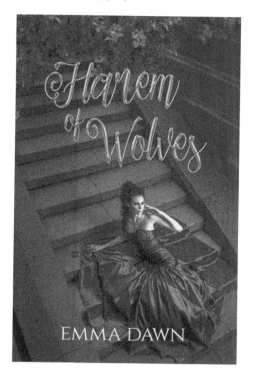

As a skydiving instructor with a black belt in karate, Cassie Denver would never have thought facing down a couple big dogs would be a problem.

But great big wolves, that turn into even larger, sexier than sin men, all who want a taste of her body? Now she has a rather delicious problem.

Surrounded by seven of the big bad wolves who all want a shot at being her Alpha in and out of her bedroom, she must choose between them if she is going to save any of them.

One night of mind blowing sex, and soul shattering pleasure with each of them.

A simple problem, with a simple solution.

Except Cassie wants every single one of those wolves on her very own leash, begging for more.

"Emma Dawn writes a laugh out loud, hang onto your panties book that will leave you panting for more."
— Early Reviewer

Learn more about me and my books at:
www.emmadawnromance.com

Or sign up for my newsletter to get the goods early!
http://eepurl.com/cG6wKL

Made in United States
North Haven, CT
11 November 2023

43885473R00124